BOOK ONE

THE FAE REALM SERIES

FATE

CATHLIN SHAHRIARY

The Fae Realm
by Cathlin Shahriary

Cover design by Indie Solutions by Murphy Rae
Formatting by Alyssa Garcia at Uplifting Designs

To Hassan,
You are my Conall, my everything. I love you.

FATE

Chapter 1

LOLA RESTED HER forehead against the chilled glass. The world outside was coated in a hazy, grey fog. She sighed, not looking forward to her stay if the weather was any indication of what was to come. She tapped on the window, drumming her chipped purple nails in a steady rhythm.

"Lola," her father warned. His growl only made her want to drum her nails harder, but she resisted the urge, pressing her fingertips forcefully into the glass in an effort to contain the angry retort dancing upon her lips. She knew it would only result in extending her prison sentence further.

She took a deep breath and seethed, "Tell me again why you think sending me to stay with a relative I hardly know is for the best."

"You know why, Lola. I work too much, and I can't trust you not to fall back into your old habits if you remain at home alone for the summer. You'll have more supervision here."

Old habits—*ha*. He wouldn't even say the words, nope, not her perfect father. He would never admit that his daughter had a drug problem. It would ruin his image of their perfect family, and he couldn't have that. Whom he was trying to fool, Lola was not sure. She hadn't exactly been discreet in her fall from grace.

About five months before, Lola had realized that no matter how hard she tried, she would never be the perfect daughter her father wanted her to be, so she stopped trying. Instead, she rebelled against unobtainable perfection. She started hiding her skinny frame in baggy t-shirts and frayed jeans from Goodwill—no more designer clothes, no more skirts, no more heels, and no more pink. She was done looking like a high school queen bee cliché. To top off her new look, she dyed her naturally pale blonde hair dark brown with blue streaks.

Unfortunately, her change in wardrobe seemingly went unnoticed by her father. While she fumed and seethed, he didn't say anything about her transformation. He chose to ignore it, hoping she would go back to the girl she had been before when she didn't get the attention she craved.

Of course, at school her supposed friends—the popular crowd who used to worship her—were quick to shun this new Lola since she no longer fit their perfect image either. Practically overnight she fell to the bottom of the social ladder, but she decided they hadn't really been her friends in the first place if they were so quick to let her go. She just needed one person to truly care about her. *Her*—not her popularity, her father's career, her clothes, her money, or her car—*only her*.

In her last attempt to fit in, she attended a house party. She remembered the music, the desire to lose herself for one night, to no longer think or feel. When a cute guy offered her an escape, she took it. She had usually abstained from drugs at parties in an effort to maintain her perfect image, but now that was no longer a concern for her. Lola quickly discovered that one little pill could make her feel free. Being high was better than the numbness she had been feeling, so she started using recreationally at the parties she attended. When one pill no longer created the euphoria she longed for, she dipped into some of the harder stuff. She knew where she was headed, but she was so desperate for someone to notice and save her from herself she just kept spiraling downward.

Shit. Just thinking about the drugs made her skin itch for a taste. Part of her still craved their effects, what they did to her system. Lola snapped an elastic band against her wrist forcefully several times. She couldn't let her thoughts or cravings control her again. She needed to be the one in control, at least in this one aspect of her life.

The car turned down a long gravel drive, yanking her from her thoughts. She took a deep, steadying breath and released it against the glass, causing the window to fog. At some point a light misting rain had started to fall outside. She tried to peer out the window at her new home for the summer, but she couldn't see anything through the gloom. The gravel crunched under the tires as the car came to a stop.

Lola's dad unbuckled his seatbelt and reached down to pull the lever, opening the trunk. With his hand on the door handle, his eyes flashed in the review mirror. He stared at Lola. For a second his gaze seemed desperate and lost, like a man at the end of his rope, but just as quickly it shifted into a hard, angry stare, as if the little girl he used to know was dead and gone, and the person who sat behind him had been the one to kill her.

"All right Lola, you know how to reach me if you need something. I expect you to not cause problems for your great-aunt. She's older and may need your help with things around the house. I'll be back to get you at the beginning of August." He paused, his scowl increasing. "This summer is your chance to prove to me that you've changed, that I can trust you alone at the house and don't need to ship you off to a boarding facility for your senior year." His angry stare softened slightly, but he quickly closed his eyes and released a pent-up sigh of resignation.

"Sure. Whatever, Dad," Lola replied, slowly unbuckling her seatbelt. She tried to play off her heartbreak as nonchalance. She would not let him see how much his words cut her. She had tried so hard for so long to be the best daughter, but it was never good enough. *She* was never good enough.

Her dad reached his limit and slammed his left hand against the steering wheel. "Damn it Lola, you really need to get your shit together. I will not put up with another year like the last one. I will not watch you destroy yourself." With that, he quickly got out of the vehicle and slammed the door shut.

Well, that was quite a change. Usually he seemed to be worried about her destroying their family image or his reputation, but he hadn't mentioned anything about Lola destroying herself before.

She huffed out the breath she hadn't even realized she was holding. *Great. Way to go, Lola. Keep this up and you may be stuck here until after graduation.* She sighed and opened the car door. The trunk slammed shut, startling her out of her thoughts and into the present. Her sneakers crunched noisily on the grey gravel drive as she walked around the car.

Her eyes flicked up at the two-story cottage that dominated the clearing at the top of a gently sloping hill. The open area almost seemed unnatural with the rest of the area thickly covered by wild forest. She drew her gaze back toward the porch. Her father stood woodenly while a woman with long grey hair attempted to hug him.

Lola had only met her great-aunt once that she could remember, and she was unsure of how things would go. She remembered that Aunt Grace had seemed like a breath of fresh air to her five-year-old self. Grace was carefree and affectionate, and it made her wonder if her mother had been the same as her aunt. Her father never liked to invite Aunt Grace over, probably because her tree-hugging hippy attire didn't match his perfect home. Also, he didn't seem to care much for anything that reminded him of Lola's mother, including Lola. It seemed like he'd rather forget her mother entirely.

Sometimes she remembered her mom and dad together as a couple. He seemed so much younger then, lighter and quicker to smile and joke. He read her stories and sometimes tucked her in at night. She remembered the time he bandaged and kissed her skinned knees after she fell trying to climb a tree. His world had revolved around their little family and working hard so he could provide for them—sometimes too hard. After her mother died, it was like a part of him died as well. He locked away everything Lola and her mom had loved about him. Maybe it was his way of dealing with grief, becoming a workaholic and avoiding interactions with the daughter who reminded him so much of the wife he lost. Sometimes Lola felt like she'd lost both parents the day they buried her mom. She was tired of reminding herself that things hadn't always been this way. It was the reason she had tried for so long to be the perfect daughter for him. She still loved him, and while he may not have said it, she knew part of him still loved her.

Her dad quickly deposited Lola's suitcases on the front

porch, thanked Aunt Grace once more, and turned to leave. He glanced at Lola briefly, meeting her eyes. She noted the sadness in them, but he didn't say a word as he got in the car. She should have been used to his behavior by now, but the disappointment still struck a chord. It felt like he couldn't get away from her fast enough. *What kind of father does that?* She closed her eyes against the spreading heartache.

"Lola, honey, come in, out of the rain," Aunt Grace called.

She opened her eyes and glanced once more toward the black sedan crunching back down the driveway. Her skin and hair were getting damp, but she didn't seem to care. As she turned toward the house, she thought she saw a man at the edge of the woods, but when she took a second glance, the mysterious figure was gone. She rubbed her hands up and down her arms to appease the goose bumps that prickled her skin and scolded herself for letting her imagination run wild. *Geez, Lola, get a grip.* She climbed the five steps to the front porch and nervously bit her lower lip.

"Lola." Her aunt sighed her name like she had been waiting for this moment for years. "Look at you. You've grown so much since I last saw you—and I should hope so, considering you were such a little thing. I don't know if you remember me, but I'm Grace, your great-aunt. You can call me Aunt Grace or Grace, whichever you prefer. Your father wouldn't tell me why he suddenly agreed to let you stay with me, but I'm sure glad he did. I've been begging him for the last decade or so to let us visit. Come in, come in. Let me show you around."

That was interesting, since her father had termed her summer as more of a punishment than a wanted vacation. He'd also certainly never mentioned the fact that he had been in contact with her Grace over the years, or that she wanted Lola to come visit. *Figures*, she thought with a snort.

She took a minute to study her aunt. Grace was probably around 5'5" with curly grey hair that almost reached down to her waist. She had many more wrinkles than Lola remembered, especially around the eyes and lips, and she wore a long, flowy, olive green skirt with a billowy flower-covered blouse. Aunt Grace pushed open the door and grabbed one of Lola's suitcases.

"Oh, I can get those," she quickly said, reaching for the luggage. She certainly didn't want to cause the older woman to have a heart attack on her first day there.

"Nonsense," replied her Aunt Grace. "I may be old, but I'm not decrepit yet!" She winked at Lola, grabbed the heaviest suitcase, and went inside. Glad to see her aunt at least had a sense of humor, she smiled. *Maybe this won't be so bad after all*, she thought.

Chapter 2

HE COTTAGE WAS really cozy on the inside. Everything looked warm and lived in, a sharp contrast to her father's pristine, modern home. She instantly liked it. She followed her great-aunt up the stairs.

"Straight ahead is the bathroom, and I'm sorry dear, but we'll have to share. To the left is your bedroom, and mine is to the right. There should be plenty of linens in your closet for the bed. Fresh towels are in the closet in the bathroom. Downstairs you'll find the living room, dining room, library, and kitchen. Feel free to help yourself to whatever you need. We can go into town tomorrow and go shopping. I didn't know what foods you liked, so I thought it might be easiest if we did that together. If there's anything else you need, just let me know. I'll let you get settled, but you're welcome to join me downstairs as I scrounge up something for us to eat for dinner."

Grace plunked Lola's suitcase down on the bed in Lola's new room and headed out the door then stopped and turned suddenly. "Oh, and I'm so glad you're here." With those words, she wrapped Lola in the biggest hug she had received in quite some time. Unsure of how to accept the affection, Lola sat stiffly in Aunt Grace's arms, but Aunt Grace didn't seem to notice at all. After a few wonderfully warm moments, Grace released her and strolled down the stairs. Lola released a shaky breath. *So this is what family is supposed to feel like.*

Lola took in her new room, which was quaint and cozy, just like the rest of the house. The walls were covered in floral wallpaper and the floors were a faded grey wood. The twin bed looked comfortable with a homemade quilt and fluffy pillows. There was a small closet as well as a white dresser with a vanity mirror. She unpacked her clothes and shoes, putting them into the dresser and closet. She took her toiletries and placed them in the bathroom, which was larger than she'd thought it would be, complete with a toilet, sink, large counter, and two white cabinets. Her favorite was the antique claw foot tub that sat off to the side against the wall. A showerhead and curtain had been added to it, but she was looking forward to a relaxing bath.

Unpacking took a lot less time than she'd expected, considering how long it had taken her to pack. She soon found herself with nothing to do, so she wandered downstairs. The living room greeted her with a warm fire in the small fireplace and blankets across the arms of the sage green sofa. She walked down the hallway finding an impressive library full of books that she couldn't wait to explore.

She heard the sound of humming as she approached the kitchen. She pushed the swinging door open as a knife clacked against a cutting board. Her aunt glanced up from chopping herbs. "Ah, wonderful! You found me. I was just finishing dinner. I hope pasta is okay." Grace smiled.

"Pasta sounds great," Lola replied, glancing around at the kitchen. It was rather large for an older house, with a butcher block island in the middle where her aunt was working. She pulled up a stool, unsure of what else to do. The silence of watching her aunt work was slightly awkward, but comfortable at the same time. A timer dinged and Grace pulled the pasta off the gas stove to drain it. She added sauce and the fresh basil she had been chopping. "It smells great," Lola complimented.

"Thank you, dear. It's your mother's favorite recipe. I used to make it all the time for her when she lived here." Lola's heart stuttered at the mention of her mother. She felt like she knew so little about her mom since her dad refused to talk about her.

"Really?" Lola asked, hoping Grace would continue.

"Oh yes. After your grandparents died in that terrible car accident, I was the one who raised Ayanna, but I'm sure you know the story." She didn't, in fact. This was the first she had heard about her grandparents' accident or her mother's childhood, but Grace continued on. "You know, you remind me a lot of her."

"I do?" God, she sounded like a puppy begging for scraps at the table.

"You look a lot like she did when she was your age. It's all in the face—your nose and the way you smile. I wish I could say she had the same gorgeous violet shade of eyes, but hers were a deep blue. The wavy hair—although she dyed it on different occasions, hers never did have blue." Grace smiled so warmly, and Lola knew her words weren't meant to be an insult. "I think she would have liked it," Grace added.

Lola genuinely smiled for the first time in months.

Those simple words were rays of sunshine to her soul. Her mother would have liked her hair. Her mother would have liked her—no, not just like, her mother would have loved her just the way she was. Her lift in spirits was tinged with sadness with the reminder that her mom wasn't there anymore. She helped Grace carry the dishes to a small table in the corner of the kitchen so they could eat.

As if sensing Lola's shift in mood, Grace spent their meal recalling many stories of her mother's mischievous childhood adventures. It was comforting to know that her mother may have been more like her than she thought. The food was delicious, so Lola could see why it was her mom's favorite meal. Several times she caught herself laughing at one of Grace's stories. It was bittersweet hearing memories of the mother she never really got to know. She yearned to hear more about her, but each memory was a reminder that her mom was gone. By the end of dinner, Lola felt more kinship toward her Aunt Grace than she had toward her father in years. Perhaps the summer wouldn't be the prison sentence she had been expecting.

CHAPTER 3

LOLA LAY IN bed that night replaying the stories she had heard over dinner. She'd enjoyed every second of listening to her mother's childhood adventures with Aunt Grace. Her mother had always been a mystery to her, a taboo topic in her house. She had tried to talk about her mom several times with her dad, but he always gave her the same response: "She's gone now. Let's leave it at that." She knew her mother had died shortly after her fifth birthday, but she struggled to remember the finer details, like her touch, her voice when she sang Lola to sleep. Sometimes she could still remember her mom's laugh, a light tinkling sound, like wind chimes. The one picture she had managed to find was all she had left of the woman who had once loved her. Now, here was her aunt who seemed to have the answers to all of her questions. She couldn't wait to learn more about her mom.

A cold chill shivered down her spine, and goose bumps broke out all over her arms and legs. She shuddered and jumped out of bed to grab an extra quilt from the closet. As she was walking back toward her bed, she glanced up at the window. The rain had stopped sometime during dinner and a bright, full moon now graced the sky. She wondered how many times her own mother had stood at that very window looking up at the moon.

Something drew her eyes away from the moon and toward the tree line at the edge of the clearing. Silhouetted there against the shadows of the forest, she saw what appeared to be man. *Impossible*, she thought. She stared, afraid to blink in case the figure disappeared. Sure enough, she could definitely make out his shape. He seemed to be leaning against a tall oak tree. It looked like that was his favorite spot and he had struck that exact pose a thousand times. She shivered again and glanced back at the moon. When she looked down, he was gone, like he had never been there. *Weird.* Lola climbed back into bed and tried to think of something other than the mysterious man at the edge of the forest who may or may not have been real, but when she finally fell asleep, he invaded her dream.

She approached the forest from the clearing wearing a flowing, deep purple gown. It seemed airy and light, clinging to her and creating curves where she didn't have any. It felt like silk against her skin, and she longed to have the dress in real life. She imagined she looked like some ethereal goddess with her pale skin contrasting with the deep purple of the dress and the shadows of the night. The moon was as full and bright as it had been when she looked out the window. It lit up the clearing so she could see fairly well as she approached the shadowy figure of the man. He was still leaning against the large oak with such casualness, and she felt awkward in comparison. "Hello, who

are you? Why are you here?" she called out.

"All questions will be answered with time. What's important is that you are here, and you are safe." His voice was like a soothing lullaby, instantly putting her at ease. As she approached him, she could tell he was slightly taller than her, which was interesting considering her above-average 5'10" height. His face, however, was covered in shadows from the oak tree. She could only make out long hair bound in a ponytail and pointed ears. Pointed ears? Okay, now she really knew she was dreaming.

"Okay, Spock. Thanks for that incredibly helpful answer." Lola's words dripped with sarcasm.

The mysterious man chuckled, and his laughter slid right down her spine to her toes, leaving a tingling sensation in its wake. She yearned to hear him laugh again. She stepped forward to get closer to him, but he seemed to retreat farther into the woods. "Not yet, milady," he said softly before slipping completely into the shadows of the woods.

Lola stood there for several minutes wondering what the hell had just happened. Disappointed and confused, she turned to head back toward the house.

Looking up from the edge of the woods, she realized she was no longer standing in her aunt's front yard. Instead she stood in the yard of a house she hoped to never see again. A large two-story colonial home loomed in the distance. The bass from music thrummed through the air, and instantly her heart raced until it threatened to burst through her chest. No. No! NO! She tried to take slow, calming breaths, but she started to hyperventilate instead.

It was the same nightmare that usually entered her sleep, the dream about the night that changed everything. She had been using drugs recreationally for a month, but this time was different. It was just a few days after she turned seventeen, and the only acknowledgement of the her birthday was a Saks Fifth Avenue gift card from her father, like she even shopped there anymore.

She went to the party hoping to escape her life once again, maybe even hook up with a guy so she could finally feel something other than the numbness that had invaded her. What Seth, her dealer, gave her was too strong this time. No longer was she feeling the rush and freedom that came with getting high; instead she started hallucinating. She could see them: ridiculously gorgeous teenagers scattered amongst the crowd, with eyes that seemed to glow and mouths full of sharp, pointed teeth. The ethereal beings were dancing with everyone, not discriminating by gender, enticing the teens around her. The crowd appeared as a mass of writhing bodies and roaming hands. She was sure if some of them didn't have clothes on, much more than dancing would be taking place. Their dance partners seemed to be drunk or high by the way they swayed and grinded against the strange imposters. They couldn't be human, not with those eyes and sharp features. This must be what a bad trip feels like, she thought to herself. This can't be real. This cannot be real.

A gorgeous boy across the dance floor stared at her while he thrust his hips against the backside of a scantily clad girl. His hands rested on the girl's bare stomach, roving from her hips to ribcage. His eyes were a glowing icy blue, his hair a spiky platinum white. His handsome face was all sharp angles and strong points. He smiled seductively, revealing sharp teeth, and he slowly ran his tongue over his the pointed tips while he maintained eye contact with her, looking much like a wolf staring at a fresh piece of meat. Lola inhaled sharply. This can't be real.

This can't be real.

He turned to whisper something in his dance partner's ear, and that was when Lola noticed his pointed ears. She rubbed her eyes as if that single action would clear her mind. I must be hallucinating, she thought. She lurched up from her seat on the couch, desperate to escape the bizarre scene around her. Her head swam and her vision blurred as she stumbled down a hallway, trying to reach a bathroom before she got sick all over the floor. She fell through the first door that would open.

Shit. Not a bathroom, but a bedroom. Lola turned to leave when she smacked into a hard body. She heard the door click shut and her heart started to race. "Where are you going, little one?" his voice whispered in her ear. She instantly felt the need to take a shower and scrub her skin raw until she could feel clean again.

"I need a bathroom," she replied nervously as she glanced up to see who she had run into. The guy with icy blue eyes and spiky platinum hair stood inches in front of her. "Excuse me," she said, hoping he would move out of the way, but he only chuckled. The sound made her stomach roll. His eyes glimmered with a mixture of mischief and malice.

"You're not going anywhere, little one. I'm not letting you go now that I found you. He will be so pleased when I tell him you're alive." The strange boy grinned. She struggled to look away from his swirling, glowing eyes. His gaze felt like ice freezing her to the core. Surely she was imagining things. Why else would he say something so strange? This couldn't be real.

This can't be real.

This cannot be real.

She kept trying to convince herself that she must be hallucinating but then the boy used his hulking frame to force her backward toward the bed. She knew then that this was worse than a bad trip. This was really happening.

"I'll scream," she threatened, trying to keep the bile from coming up out of her throat. She knew there was a slim chance someone would hear her over the music, but she didn't know what else to do. It seemed the boy also knew she was unlikely to be heard over the party outside the room since a smile crept across his mouth, exposing the tips of his sharp teeth.

"Go ahead," he challenged. His eyes narrowed as he shoved her down onto the bed. He crawled on top of her using his weight to pin her down until he was straddling her. His hands held her wrists captive against the mattress. When she kicked her legs to shake his embrace, he gripped her wrists painfully tighter. "I'll just have a little taste before we go. He doesn't have to know," he continued, as if her struggle made it all the more sweet. His words confused her, but she quickly lost focus when his tongue snaked out and licked the column of her throat. The instant his tongue touched her skin, something inside her snapped. Lola screamed for all she was worth. She thrashed her entire body, arms and legs flailing as much as they could. She was not going to just let this happen. She was going to fight.

"Wake up, milady..." A soft, out-of-place voice whispered in her head. It didn't belong here. It wasn't part of her memory.

Lola awoke with a start, sitting straight up in bed with the sheets tangled around her. Her heart pounded as she gasped for breath. She could still feel his breath on her skin. Her hands rubbed her neck, trying to erase the memory of the attack. She hated that nightmare, and it never failed to haunt her. Her therapist said that over time, the nightmares would lessen and hopefully cease if she could work through her issues.

She glanced down at her wrists as if she could still see the faint bruises from his grip. Her hands shook as she tried to calm her racing heart, her mind spinning as she thought back to the event that changed her life. The worst part from that night was she didn't know what was real and what was a result of the drugs she had taken. It had all felt incredibly real, and someone at the party had heard her scream. When they found her, Lola was still screaming and thrashing, but her attacker had disappeared—if there had even been one to begin with. Unsure of what drugs she was on, her rescuer called an ambulance, and she had to be strapped down to the gurney by paramedics. She was still thrashing and screaming when they pulled into the hospital, where they gave her a sedative to knock her out. When she awoke later, the doctor explained that the drugs in her system must have caused a severe hallucinogenic reaction. He told her someone at the party had found her, and none of her attack had been real. She was found alone in the room fighting a ghost, so to speak.

Her father wouldn't even look at her. He stood in the corner of the hospital room with his arms crossed, glaring at the floor. When the doctor suggested treatment, her father was quick to send her off to the first rehab facility that would take her. He didn't want anyone to know what had happened, so he called the school and told them she had mono. To everyone else, he acted like nothing was wrong with his daughter. *His* daughter would never need to go to rehab. *His* daughter would have never even thought of doing drugs in the first place. After all, if a CEO can't even control his daughter, how is he supposed to control a company?

Finally her heart rate returned to normal and her hands stopped trembling. Rehab had been good for her. She had been clean for 58 days now and never wanted to lose control like that again. It had felt so real. She shivered with the memory, trying not to relive the nightmare once again. She sharply snapped the green rubber band she wore around her wrist several times to bring herself back to the present and took deep, calming breaths. *Breathe in. Breathe out. It wasn't real. It was just a dream. It didn't happen. It wasn't real.*

Chapter 4

WHEN LOLA HAD calmed down and the shaking had stopped, she glanced at the clock by her bed: 6:00 AM. She figured she might as well start the day, afraid if she tried to go back to sleep she would only end up repeating her nightmare. She listened for the sounds of her aunt to see if she was up too, but the house was silent. Lola crept downstairs, careful not to wake her aunt, and ended up in the library. Maybe reading would help calm her nerves. She curiously eyed the mahogany shelves full of books both old and new. There was a shelf full of tomes on herbs, herbal remedies, homeopathic treatments, and holistic medicines. Another shelf held a wide selection of fantasy books. Those might be interesting. She looked more closely at the titles—*A Field Guide to the Fae Realm*, *The Gift of Sight*, *Fae Folklore and Legends*, *Fairies Walk Among Us*, and *Encyclopedia of Fae*. The titles went on and on. Apparently her great-aunt really liked fairies. While she enjoyed a good paranormal read now and then, she was more of a shifter and vampire kind of girl. She kept perusing the shelves, but Fae and mythical folklore seemed to be a common theme throughout the library. Maybe it was what she did for a living. Lola couldn't remember her father mentioning what her aunt had done before she retired, and she hadn't remembered to ask the night before.

A voice spoke from the doorway and Lola jumped, startled.

"I see you discovered the library."

"Oh, yeah—I hope it's okay that I'm in here." She smiled sheepishly.

"Of course, dear. You're welcome to read anything on my shelves. In fact, you may find some of them rather informative," Grace proclaimed. "Would you like something for breakfast? I was thinking about making us some eggs and toast before we get ready and head into town. How does that sound?"

"Sounds great. Thanks," Lola agreed.

They ate breakfast and talked about what groceries to buy at the store, including what meals Lola might like. She asked Grace about her mother's favorite meals and Grace was eager to share what she used to cook for Ayanna. They came up with a menu for the upcoming week as well as a list of what they needed.

After getting showered and dressed, they hopped into Aunt Grace's old blue Chevy truck and headed into town. The town itself was rather small with just a diner, a single school for all grades, one gas station, a couple thrift and antique shops, and a grocery store. Grace explained that if Lola wanted to go to the mall or see a movie they would have to drive to the next largest town, about 30 miles away, but it wasn't that much of a bother.

She wondered if her mother had liked living at Grace's house. *Did she like the small town, or did she prefer the city?* Her thoughts about her mom experiencing the same things she was experiencing at that moment made her smile the whole time they were out. She yearned for a connection with her mom. She imagined Ayanna probably had loved it there. It was very peaceful, and based on what little she could recall of her mother, she didn't seem like a city girl.

Frequently during their shopping trip, Aunt Grace would find small ways to touch Lola, as if reassuring herself that she was indeed real and there with her. It seemed that whenever Lola glanced at Grace, she had a genuine smile and warmth in her expression that brought back memories of the way her mother used to look at her. It had been so long since she had felt such love and affection.

On the ride back from the store, Lola decided to ask Aunt Grace about the library. "So, I was looking at the books in the library and noticed you have a lot of interesting titles. What did you used to do before you retired?"

"I was an herbal healer of sorts. Still am, I suppose," Grace answered vaguely.

"What does an herbal healer do? " Lola questioned.

"Oh, I was sort of like a homeopathic doctor for the townsfolk. I studied which natural herbs or medicines could help which illnesses and diseases, and I would help the people who needed those remedies. I studied plants and diet as well as other elements of nature that may be able to help," Grace explained.

"So is all the Fae folklore stuff a hobby? I noticed quite a few of those books in your library," Lola probed.

"Those were your mother's," Grace stated.

"My mother's?" Lola was shocked.

"Yes, she studied folklore and myths in college. The fairy stories always interested her as a child, so she decided to turn the hobby into something more when she went off to school," Grace explained.

"Aunt Grace, what happened to my mother exactly? It's just…Dad refuses to talk about her."

"Oh, sweetheart. Your mother was a wonderful woman, but she had a lot of hardships in her life. She had you when she was rather young, but she was so happy. You were the center of her little world. She tried so hard to escape her problems, but they always seemed to follow her. I guess one day she just gave up and accepted the darkness she had allowed to seep into her life." Grace sighed.

"What do you mean she just gave up and accepted the darkness?" Lola's voice trembled with uncertainty. Did she really want to know the truth, even if it meant her mom might have been unstable?

"We aren't sure exactly," Grace answered. Even though Aunt Grace faced the windshield, Lola noticed the guilt playing across her features. What was she not telling her? "Your father was the one who found her. He came home and found you crying in the hallway. When he went to look for your mother, she was frantically packing clothes into a suitcase, muttering about someone coming for her. When your father tried to talk to her, she wouldn't respond to him. She just kept throwing things into the suitcase, mumbling about them coming for her and saying she couldn't let them find you. He tried to shake her out of it, but she fainted the minute he put his hands on her. He called 911, of course. I think he thought she was having a panic attack or accidently mixed some meds. She was rushed to the hospital, but she never regained consciousness and was in a coma for three weeks before she finally let go.

"Your father later confessed that Ayanna seemed to be paranoid the month before her episode. She started refusing to go outside or let you play outside. He was beyond devastated, which is why I'm sure he doesn't talk about her passing with you, but it breaks my heart to know he doesn't talk about her at all. He loved her so completely, and it shattered him to lose her. Unfortunately, for some people it's just easier to try to forget than to live with the pain." Grace placed a comforting hand on Lola's knee as she drove.

This was so much worse than she'd thought. Lola had always imagined that maybe her mom had died in a car accident or had some medical condition, not that she went crazy. She struggled to understand exactly what had happened.

"What caused her coma?" Lola whispered, thinking aloud.

Grace sighed deeply. "Your father and the doctors believe it was exhaustion or some sort of mental illness or trauma."

"But you don't." That was Lola's guess, based on her aunt's tone.

"No, sweetheart, I don't. I refuse to believe your mother was mentally ill. I just think there are some things in this world we can't explain, and it can become too much to bear." Grace's features were full of sorrow and understanding as she finished her explanation. Her tone indicated that she didn't want to talk about it anymore, and Lola was okay with that. She didn't want to think about her mother being crazy either—it was too heartbreaking and disappointing—although a history of mental illness might explain some of her own issues. Maybe her problems were hereditary.

CHAPTER 5

WHEN LOLA WENT to her bedroom that evening, she took a book with her. Perhaps it would help to have something to read when she woke up from the nightmare again. She grabbed a random Fae book, finding comfort in knowing it had once belonged to her mother. She could imagine her mom reading the same book late at night in her room. She changed into a tank top and shorts and was getting ready to climb into bed when she felt a pull toward the window. She glanced out at the moon. It was partially hidden behind clouds, but still bright and relatively full. She sighed at its beauty and felt her eyes being drawn downward. As she searched the tree line surrounding the clearing, her breath caught.

He was there again, leaning against that same oak tree. In the light of morning she had completely forgotten about him, but she made a mental note to ask her aunt about any neighbors the next day. She also wondered why she didn't feel freaked out by his presence. "I'm sure most girls love a good stalker. Way to attract the creepers, Lola," she whispered to herself, oozing sarcasm. She reached down to snap her elastic to make sure the moment was in fact real and he wasn't a hallucination. The rubber band stung her wrist, and still he remained. Abruptly he turned and faded into the forest.

"Get it together. Quit thinking about creepy stalkers outside your window," she muttered. She sat down on her bed with the book in hand. She tried to think about what she already knew about Fae or fairies. Of course, Tinker-bell was what first came to mind. She had read other supernatural books, but more along the lines of vampires and werewolves like *Twilight* and *The Grey Wolves* series by Quinn Loftis. *Wait...* Now that she thought about it, *The Grey Wolves* books had Fae in them—beautiful human like creatures that lived in another realm and had magical powers. Then there was *Supernatural*. She loved Sam and Dean Winchester (talk about yummy), and she seemed to recall an episode with Charlie and LARPing where a fairy was being used by a human. Again, magical powers and beauty seemed to be a theme. She looked at the cover of the book in her hands: *A Field Guide to the Fae Realm*. That seemed like a good place to start.

She flipped open the well-worn cover and gasped. There was her mother's name in swirling blue ink. The handwriting was a feminine loopy cursive, and she traced each of the letters with her fingertip. She felt connected to her mom in that moment. Deciding she was too tired to read that evening, she hugged the book to her chest and lay down to sleep.

She was in the clearing again, wearing the same gorgeous,

deep purple gown. Her hair was down past her shoulders, waves fluttering in the breeze that stirred the air. She approached the forest tentatively. She couldn't see him leaning against the oak tree, but she felt his presence. The goose bumps prickled up her arms. "I know you're there. Why don't you want to show yourself tonight?" she called to the trees. She was proud of herself for being so brave, but the truth was she was too curious not to find him. Of course, he could be some psycho stalker for all she knew, but she still felt completely safe. It was rather disconcerting.

"Hello again, milady." His rich voice covered her like a warm blanket. "I did not want to scare you."

"Scare me? Why would you scare me?"

"Well, after I saw you last night, you had terrible dreams. I was afraid it was because of me," he explained, stepping forward a bit. This time she could see that his hair was dark—brown or black, perhaps—and wavy, but pulled back into a ponytail that fell a little past his shoulders. His face was still partially covered by shadows, but she could make out his pointed ears and muscular build. He was wearing what looked like soft leather pants, boots, and a tight shirt. She wished she could see his face.

"Why don't you come closer? I won't bite, Spock... well, at least not too hard," she teased.

He chuckled, and the glorious sound filled her with warmth again. "I don't think that would be wise." The disappointment settled like a stone in her stomach. Why wouldn't he let her see his face? Was he hideous? Was it like the Phantom of the Opera over there? Did he look like Sloth from The Goonies? She didn't believe it. The rest of him was so deliciously appealing. He must have seen the disappointment written on her face. "Don't worry. We will meet again soon."

"Meet? But we have met. I'm talking to you now," Lola puzzled.

"Yes, but only in your dreams. While I enjoy our time together in here, I would like to see you up close in person. Meet me by the tall oak tomorrow night. I will be there," he replied. *Then just like that, he faded into the shadows.*

Lola turned to walk back into her aunt's house when she realized the setting had shifted and she was standing outside the party house again. No. No! She didn't want to go in there. She didn't want to relive it yet again. Her whole body started to tremble, but her feet seemed to move without her permission. She saw flashes of sharp teeth, glowing ice blue eyes.

Suddenly a hand grabbed her wrist. It was warm and gentle. "Wake up," a soothing, familiar voice urged her in her ear.

Lola blinked her eyes open. Her breathing was slightly labored, but her heart beat at a normal rhythm. She had woken up before the nightmare could start. For the first time in over two months, she had been able to pull herself out of the dream before it had begun. She released a slow, calming breath. Surely her therapist would agree that this was a momentous event.

She crept down to the kitchen to get a glass of water. From the window over the kitchen sink, she glanced outside. Amongst the trees she thought she saw a flash of teeth and glowing eyes. Her heart stopped and she froze in fear. A few heartbeats later, cold water coated her hand from the overflowing glass, pulling her out of her shock. She glanced down and turned off the sink. She peeked back at the window—nothing. She must have imagined it. It couldn't be real. She snapped the band around her wrist and took a couple of deep, calming breaths. When she raised her glass to her lips to take a sip, she realized her hands were still trembling. She cautiously climbed the stairs back to her bedroom with her glass of water. She set the glass on her bedside table and picked up *A Field Guide to the Fae Realm*. She read the introduction and first chapter about the history of Fae before her eyes started drooping and she couldn't keep them open any longer. It wasn't long before sharp teeth and icy eyes invaded her calm and she found herself waking again.

CHAPTER 6

THE NEXT MORNING at breakfast, Lola decided to bring up the man from the forest. "Aunt Grace, do you have any neighbors close by?" she started.

"Oh no, dear. My closest neighbors live probably five miles down the hill, a sweet older couple. We have quite a bit of woodland surrounding us as well as farmland. Why do you ask?"

Well, there goes that theory. She didn't know what to make of the man from the forest and was afraid to ask in case he wasn't real. "Do you think I could go explore the woods today?" she asked hopefully, deflecting her aunt's question.

"I think that's a wonderful idea. Just be careful. There are dangerous things that live in those woods and it's easy to get lost. I wouldn't venture far from the clearing, okay?" Grace requested.

Lola didn't want to upset the one person who had been so nice to her and treated her like real family, so she agreed to stay close to the house.

Outside, she strolled across the grassy clearing. She glanced up at the sky, which was a clear blue. She almost felt like having a *Sound of Music* moment and spinning around on the hill with her arms spread wide. She could hear the song in her mind: *The hills are alive with the sound of music...aaaahhh...aahhh...aahhh.* She was so busy looking up at the sky that she hadn't realized how close she had walked to the tree line. She approached it cautiously, listening for sounds of wild animals or mysterious men. Nothing seemed out of the ordinary, so she continued.

She stepped into the shade of the tall oak tree and placed her hand against its bark, closing her eyes. He stood here in her dream. She could see him perfectly in her mind, minus his shadowed face. She opened her eyes and glanced down toward the base of the trunk. There, sitting on the grass beside the tall oak was a vibrant, violet flower. It was stunning, the shape of its petals unlike any flower she had seen before. Its slender stem had been cut, not plucked, and it seemed as if someone had left it there intentionally, but that couldn't be right. She brought its violet petals up to her nose and inhaled deeply. Its delicate fragrance filled the air. She sighed audibly, releasing the floral scent. She tucked the flower behind her ear for safe-keeping and stepped farther into the woods.

There was so much shade that it was relatively cool in the forest, slightly chillier than it had been in the clearing. There were trees of varying heights and wildflowers of red, orange, and lavender blooming. She found a patch of wild blackberries and picked a few. They were juicy and sweet on her lips. "Lola? Lola, honey, where are you?" She could hear her aunt calling her. She plucked one more blackberry and turned to walk back into the clearing. Out of the corner of her eye she caught a glimpse of icy blue. Her heart skipped a beat and she suddenly found herself sprinting out of the woods and into the clearing.

"Oh there you are," Grace commented. "Is everything okay? You look a little pale."

"I thought I…I thought I saw… Never mind," Lola stammered, trying to catch her breath.

"What do you think you saw, dear?" Grace inquired. "It's okay to tell me. I may understand more than you know."

"It was nothing, Aunt Grace. Don't worry."

After all, Lola hadn't really stuck around to see if it was anything. It could have been her imagination running wild again. She thought she saw the icy blue-eyed boy everywhere.

"Okay, sweetheart. Lunch is ready if you're hungry. Did you find anything interesting while you were exploring?" Aunt Grace chatted as she walked back toward the cottage with Lola.

"Some delicious blackberries—oh, and this flower," she replied, pointing to the violet bloom tucked behind her ear.

"Well isn't that just perfect?" Aunt Grace lilted, but her face seemed a little tight, a crease forming between her eyes. She shook her head as if to throw off whatever worry was there for a moment then pressed on as if nothing was out of the ordinary. "A violet flower for a violet flower." She must have seen the puzzled look on Lola's face because she continued. "Your first name, Ianthe—didn't your father tell you where your name came from?"

Lola shook her head no. The only time she could recall hearing her first name aloud was with her mother's fading voice. Her father and everyone else had always called her by her middle name, Lola. When she asked her father about her first name, he said her mother had given it to her, but it was too strange and difficult for most people to pronounce. Besides, she was named Lola after his grandmother and that should be good enough. She accepted his explanation because—let's face it—most kids or teachers wouldn't look at Ianthe and pronounce it eye-AN-thee.

Grace explained, "Your mother wanted to name you Ianthe after taking one look into those beautiful violet eyes. Ianthe means violet flower in Greek. I think it was also a way of keeping you close to her. Do you know what Ayanna means?" Lola shook her head, and Grace smiled fondly. "It means beautiful flower. I think it was her way of passing on her name to you. Your father wasn't a huge fan of Ianthe, but your mother insisted, so she gave you the middle name Lola, after his mother, to appease him. She always called you her little Ianthe. I think she may have been a little hurt when your father told everyone your name was Lola. I'm surprised you didn't know where your name came from. Although, if your father doesn't ever talk about your mother..." Grace paused slightly before continuing, "Haven't you ever wondered, dear?"

Of course I've wondered! Lola wanted to yell. *I've wondered a whole hell of a lot of things, like what my mother's favorite color was and if she ever sang in the shower.* She snapped her elastic and took a calming breath. She couldn't get mad at Aunt Grace. It wasn't Grace's fault she knew nothing about her mother. It was her father's silence that left her missing pieces of herself. Did he know what he was doing by refusing to tell her anything about her mother? Did he know how much it affected her? Apparently Aunt Grace sensed the shift in Lola's emotion because she quickly changed gears. "Come on, dear. Let's get lunch before it gets too late." With those words, she walked up the steps to the cottage, leaving Lola to pull herself together and follow her inside.

CHAPTER 7

AFTER A COMFORTABLY silent lunch, Lola helped Aunt Grace collect herbs for her medicines and tinctures. It was interesting to learn the names of the different plants as well as their medicinal properties. As the sun began to set, butterflies fluttered in Lola's stomach any time she remembered the mysterious dream man's invitation for a meeting. A nervous energy infused her body, making it hard to sit still. Even Aunt Grace noticed, although she didn't know the cause. She assumed Lola was starting to get anxious because they had yet to hear from her father. Lola would have bet fifty bucks they wouldn't hear from him for at least a few weeks. It wasn't like she and her father really communicated while she was home, only small snippets of sentences and slamming doors.

At dinner Grace told her more stories about little Ayanna and teenage Ayanna, who had been known to sneak off into the woods and meet boys at night. *Hmmm...maybe we're more alike than I thought.* She could feel that Grace was trying to tiptoe around conversation with her, and Lola was great at listening but not really adding to the conversation. Her mind had started to drift to a certain tall, dark, and mysterious man then she realized her aunt had been asking her a question and waiting for her to answer.

"I'm sorry, what?" she asked.

"Oh dear, not you too." Grace laughed. "Your mother was a constant daydreamer. I used to tease her mercilessly about dreaming of her fairy stories, and she would blush from head to toe. I think part of her yearned for a little magic in this world. I asked if you found the book you borrowed interesting."

"Um, yeah I guess. I actually didn't get all that far before I fell asleep," Lola admitted.

"Well, after raising Ayanna on those stories, I know them pretty well. So, if you have any questions or want to talk about them with me, feel free," Grace encouraged.

"Okay, sure. I'm going to head up to bed and read then. Good night, Aunt Grace," she stated, turning toward the stairs. Once she reached the bedroom, she changed into her pajamas and went through the motions of getting ready for bed. The butterflies returned with a vengeance, rioting in her gut. *Am I really going to do this? Am I really going to sneak out of my room to see if the mysterious dude is real? Obviously he won't be the same one I dreamed of—that would be ridiculous.* She doubted her own sanity for leaving the comforts of the cottage to chase after figures in the night, but she had to know if he was real and make sure she wasn't still seeing things that weren't there. Now that she knew about her mother, she wanted to make sure she wasn't going crazy too.

She heard her aunt getting ready for bed and made sure to 'accidently' bump into her in the hallway getting a glass of water so she would see that Lola was indeed going to sleep. After the nighttime silence settled on the house and she was sure her aunt was asleep, she changed clothes, throwing on a pair of jeans and a Star Wars t-shirt. She pulled her hair up into a messy bun and took a deep breath to calm her nerves. Snapping the elastic sharply against her wrist, she exhaled and crept downstairs cautiously, pausing every so often to make sure she wasn't heard. When she reached the door, she slid on a pair of flip-flops. Finally she opened the door slowly, praying it wouldn't creak, and slipped out into the night.

The moon greeted her from high in the sky, casting a glow across the clearing. She could see slightly less white of the moon than the night before as it had started waning. She closed the door gently behind her and decided to jump down over the side of the porch instead of taking the steps because she knew they would creak. She landed on the grass with a silent thud and walked around the driveway to avoid the crunch of the gravel. There in the distance, she could see the tall oak tree.

As she strolled across the clearing, her eyes adjusted to the moonlight and her ears took in the sounds of the forest at night, noisy insects creating harmonies of their own music. A slight breeze rustled the leaves of the trees as her feet swished through the grass. She looked down frequently to make sure she didn't trip and hurt herself and glanced up as she closed the distance to the oak, but she didn't see her mysterious man. Disappointment burned in her throat like acid and she mentally kicked herself for being so stupid as to think he could possibly be real. She paused, debating whether to continue on toward the tree or go back to the house and wallow in self-pity. In that moment, the hairs on the back of her neck prickled. She could feel someone watching her from the woods. She took a few steps closer to the old oak and softly called out, "Hello?"

"You came," his voice responded from the darkness, making her skin tingle. She snapped her elastic against her wrist, so wanting this moment to be real.

He appeared from amidst the shadows of the forest. He was exactly as she'd pictured him in her dreams. His dark shoulder-length hair was tied back into a loose ponytail, and he was even wearing the same outfit—boots, leather pants, and a tightfitting shirt that showed off his muscles impeccably. He emanated danger, but somehow Lola was only soothed by his presence. She yearned to get closer and took a few more steps toward the tall oak. This time she could clearly see that his ears were indeed pointed. She followed the contours of his chiseled jaw and pointed nose toward his eyes, which seemed to glow the green of newborn grass in spring. Her breath caught. Being up close to him literally took her breath away. She had never seen a man so gorgeous before. All those guys she'd thought were hot before couldn't hold a candle to him. She snapped her elastic more forcibly against her wrist, the pain affirming that she indeed was awake and was not dreaming up the magnificent specimen standing in front of her. He glanced down toward her wrist as his lips tugged down into a scowl.

"Why do you hurt yourself?" he asked.

She opened her mouth, but no sound came out. It was suddenly dry. She closed her mouth and licked her lips, hoping to make her voice work this time. His eyes tracked her every movement and seemed to darken when they settled on her glistening lips. "I, um, wanted to make sure you were real," she whispered. *Wow, Lola, way to sound like an idiot.* "I'm sorry. You, um—you just look exactly as I imagined, as if I dreamed you up," she quickly added. *Oh, great, now you sound like the creepy stalker*, Lola thought, cringing inwardly. "The rubber band, um, helps me know what's real and focus in on the moment at hand." *Whew. There, maybe that will be an acceptable answer.*

His frown didn't ease, but he reached out and gently stroked her wrist where her elastic had left a red mark. "I don't like it," he stated simply. Lola just stared at his face, savoring the trail of heat his thumb left with every pass over her wrist.

After a few moments, she seemed to shake herself out of her hormone-induced stupor and yanked her hand out of his. She took a step back. "Okay, Spock, enough with the touchy feely. Who are you and why are you hanging out outside my window?"

"Who is Spock?" he asked, scrunching his eyebrows in confusion.

"You know, Spock—from Star Trek," Lola replied. She could tell he wasn't getting it as his brow remained furrowed. "The one with the pointed ears." She held up her hand, moving middle and pointer finger together as well as her ring finger and pinky. "You know, the 'live long and prosper' thing." He still looked confused, but Lola was at a loss for how to explain the connection further. "Okay, well you still didn't answer my questions."

"I am Conall," he replied, extending his hand for her to take. His eyes studied her curiously with a slight furrow between his brows. The instant she touched his skin again, it was like she was drunk on his touch. She leaned forward and closed her eyes, surrendering to the sensation. A sense of calm and rightness filled her bones as she took a deep breath. It came out as a breathy sigh. She felt a tug and realized this time she was the creeper holding on too long. He removed his hand from her grasp and she instantly missed his touch.

Stupid, stupid, Lola, she chided herself. Get a grip,

girl. Don't act like some lovesick puppy. What's wrong with you?

"I've been waiting outside your window because I was told to watch for you," he continued.

Anger sparked inside Lola instantly. *Watch for me?! Oh. My. God. My dad must have hired this guy as some sort of surveillance to make sure I stay on the straight and narrow.* "Did my dad hire you?" she barked. "I don't need anyone to watch me. I'm just fine on my own, and I don't even want to think about going back down the path I was on that landed me in here in the first place, so you can tell that overbearing son of a bitch to back off." As she finished the last part, she realized she was yelling and instantly took a few calming breaths. Her hands had unconsciously clenched into fists and her nails were slowly biting into her skin.

Conall looked taken aback. He put his hands up to appease her. "No, no. You misunderstood me. I've never met your father before."

"Oh right, you just talked to him over the phone, is that it?" she snapped in her enraged state.

"Calm down, milady. You are mistaken," Conall soothed.

"My lady? I am not *your* lady! I'm not *your* anything!" she spat.

"Of course," Conall sighed as his face fell and his eyes filled with sorrow. Lola immediately felt horrible. She hadn't meant to take her anger out on him. It wasn't his fault her father had hired him. She really needed to stop misdirecting her anger at others. He was just doing his job. It was her mistake for hoping for something more.

"Look, I'm sorry my father hired you, all right, but I

don't need watching. You can just go back to him and get him to pay you for the work you put in, but you're done. Got it? No more loitering outside my window at night." With that she turned and stomped back toward the house. It was not how she had planned her evening would go at all.

CHAPTER 8

THANKFULLY HER AUNT didn't wake up to her stomping angrily up the stairs. She changed back into her pajamas and walked to the window. It seemed Conall had listened to her and left. The feeling was bittersweet. She shoved *A Field Guide to the Fae Realm* off her bed in a huff. She just wanted to climb under the sheets and forget the night had happened at all. *Why did he have to be working for my father? How could I have not seen it before? Why did he have to be so yummy?* She wanted to scream in frustration. *I should have known he wouldn't be genuinely interested in me. I'm not anything special. Well, forget it.* She wasn't going to spend any more time thinking about that ass-clown. He didn't deserve her thoughts, or her anger. She pulled the covers up tightly under her chin and shut her eyes.

A groan escaped her lips as she realized she stood in the

clearing outside her aunt's cottage. *What is it with these dreams?* She turned to go toward the house, but no matter how far she walked in that direction, it remained the same distance away. She stomped her foot and released the yell she had been keeping inside when she fell asleep. "AAAHHH!" she bellowed as loudly as she could.

"Feel better?" His honeyed voice caused her to shiver.

She didn't want him there, damn it.

"No, I don't, as a matter of fact," she hissed.

"I'm sorry I upset you. I didn't imagine our meeting going that way at all."

"You and me both, buddy."

"You left before I could explain—"

She put her hand up to stop him. "No need, Spock. I'm pretty sure I have things all figured out just fine on my own."

"But you don't," Conall corrected. "I don't work for your father. I serve someone else. I was asked to watch the house and let him know when you were there."

"So someone else wants to know when I'm at my aunt's house?" Lola asked incredulously. "Great, well you can tell whoever you work for to leave me the hell alone, and you know what else? I am so tired of your cryptic answers. Can't you just be straightforward? What is it about me that attracts the crazies?" She hadn't realized she said the last part out loud until she heard his musical laugh. Instantly she felt an intense need to make him laugh again. She quickly tamped down that sensation and shoved it aside. She didn't have time to be attracted to a guy who was only watching her as an assignment from his boss. "Who hired you then?"

Conall looked like he was expecting her to know the

answer already. "You truly can't think of anyone who would want me to watch you?" he asked suspiciously.

Her memory flashed to icy blue eyes. Surely he didn't know who she was and wouldn't be able to find her out there. He was just some random guy from a random party. "N-No," she stuttered. "Should I?"

Conall wouldn't look her in the eye. She heard him mutter under his breath "That isn't possible...must be lying... or perhaps memories were erased." He shook his head as if to clear it, and it made a few strands of hair fall loose from his ponytail. Lola's fingers itched to tuck them behind his ear. She yearned to know if his hair was as silky as she imagined. His conversation with himself interrupted her thoughts. "She should know. Something isn't right."

"Look, I don't know what you're going on about, but I'm starting to get a little weirded out by all of this. Why would some guy I don't know hire you? What does he look like?" She said the last part almost as an afterthought.

"How would knowing what he looks like help you?"

"I don't know...I'm just trying to figure it out. Maybe I've seen him before," Lola replied.

"How old are you?"

"Seventeen."

"Are you sure?" He raised his left eyebrow in the cutest way.

"Of course I'm sure. It's my age. If I was going to lie about it, I would make myself eighteen or twenty-one, not seventeen," she huffed, annoyed.

Now it was his turn to look confused. He started pacing, conversing with himself under his breath. She just caught snippets: "Should be older...face looks just like I remember...wrong color...could be dyed." He approached her again more quickly than she thought possible. He tugged her into a patch of moonlight and tipped her chin up to meet his stormy gaze. He gasped sharply and his hands flinched away from her face as if she burned him. "This can't be." He came to a stop in front of her. "I have to go speak with someone. Will you be okay without me here for a few days?" he asked, meeting her gaze. She could get lost in his eyes—wild and green like the forest around them.

"Of course—I'm not an invalid. I did have a life I was living perfectly fine before you came along, you know, so don't assume I'm just going to sit here twiddling my thumbs with baited breath until you return. You don't even have to come back. I don't care," she lied. The corner of his mouth tugged down and she thought he looked disappointed by her response. She mentally high-fived herself. She didn't need him. This whole situation was just confusing and adding to her questionable mental state.

"I'm sorry you feel that way." He sighed then turned and disappeared into the woods without a second glance.

The low sound of bass filled the air around her and the scene shifted as she turned. She couldn't escape the nightmare in front of her. What was wrong with her? It wasn't like she wanted to keep reliving the same tortuous event over and over. She clenched her fists, digging her nails into her skin and willing herself to wake up. Her hand went automatically for the rubber band on her wrist, but it was missing. She bit down hard on her lip and tasted blood, willing some pain to shock her system into waking up. I don't want to be here. This isn't real. It isn't real. Unfortunately, no matter how hard she chanted and hoped, it was real, and she had to relive that night once again, every stupid decision and terrifying moment.

Lola awoke with a scream and her door flew open. "Lola, honey, are you okay?" Her great-aunt rushed through the doorway. She approached the bed cautiously, sat down, and stroked a comforting hand through Lola's hair. "It's okay sweetie, must have been some bad dream," she soothed.

"You have no idea," Lola murmured.

"Do you want to talk about it?"

"Not really. I just keep having the same nightmare over and over again. It always feels so real." Lola shivered, shaking off a chill that had invaded her body. "Aunt Grace, do you think it's possible to experience something other people tell you wasn't real?" Lola asked cautiously.

"If it felt real to you, then it was real, dear. It's all about our own perception of events. Just because other people may tell you it didn't happen, that doesn't mean it didn't happen to you. You obviously experienced something traumatizing if you keep having nightmares about it. Your dad was very tight-lipped about his reasons for finally agreeing to let you stay with me, and I'm starting to see why. Just know, dear, that if you ever want to talk about anything, I'm here for you," Grace said comfortingly.

While Lola was touched and felt comfortable with Aunt Grace, she didn't want to tell anyone else about what she thought had happened that night, at least not right then. "It's okay. I'm okay now. I don't really want to talk about it yet, but thank you for the offer." She smiled weakly.

"Well, since we're both up, I guess I'll make us an early breakfast." Grace hugged Lola and got up from the bed. She stumbled for a second and bent over to pick something up off the floor. "Here, dear. This may come in handy," she added as she handed Lola *A Field Guide to the Fae Realm*.

CHAPTER 9

THE NEXT TWO weeks passed in a pleasant routine for Lola. She helped Aunt Grace with whatever she needed around the house, they cooked meals together, and she learned so much about herbs and herbal remedies. She learned that Grace sold some of her tinctures and medicines at a local shop in town that had candles, books, and antique jewelry. Keeping busy helped her not to focus on any cravings for a high. Lola found that knowing herbal remedies instead of depending on pills gave her a sense of control over her addiction. She also discovered that the more time she spent with Aunt Grace, the less she wanted to escape her reality. She was staring to enjoy the here and now.

Some days the hazy grey that had filled the sky her first day there returned and brought rain, trapping Lola inside. Other days the sky was a clear blue that made everything feel electric and new. The grass was a bright green from the rain and the forest looked like it had sprung to life. Lola spent time wandering around the property gathering herbs for her aunt or picking berries, though she was always cautious not to travel too far into the woods for fear of getting lost.

It didn't take her long to find her aunt's computer and get on the internet. She showed Grace how they could watch Netflix through the computer and introduced her to her favorite show, *Supernatural*. Aunt Grace seemed to be just as intrigued by the fantastical stories of the show as well as developing a growing crush on Castiel. Lola was really enjoying her time with her aunt and it didn't feel like a punishment at all, although she could see why her dad would think so. The old Lola would have hated every minute of being out in the rural woods. The old Lola would have thrown a fit to be without TV and texting with her 'friends' every day, but she wasn't that girl anymore. His form of punishment certainly showed how little her father knew about her. He had called once, actually sooner than she would have thought, but he only spoke to Aunt Grace. She was unexpectedly disappointed, a small part of her still hoping to earn the affections of her father.

The only change had been Conall. She hadn't dreamed of him again since the night he said he would be gone. She would find herself staring out the windows toward the tall oak, searching for him, only to be crestfallen when she should have felt relieved not to find him there. Unfortunately, since she wasn't dreaming of meeting with Conall, her nightmares became the only thing that occupied her mind at night. She often got little sleep or woke up screaming. Aunt Grace would come in and comfort her on those nights, and thankfully she understood that Lola still didn't want to talk about it.

One day while reading *A Field Guide to the Fae Realm*, things started to click in place in Lola's mind. Thinking she may have seen Fae at the party, she turned to her Aunt

Grace and asked, "Do you think Fae are real?"

"Your mother certainly did," Grace smiled.

"She did?" Lola was now as curious as ever.

"Why do you ask, dear?"

Lola figured now was a good as time as any to start talking about what she had told her therapists. "Well, this might sound crazy, but I think I may have seen some of them. I mean, I was at a party a few months ago, and I saw something. I wasn't in the best state of mind to begin with"—she didn't want to admit to the drug use to her aunt, couldn't stomach disappointing the one family member who seemed to genuinely care about her—"but this was something I had never seen before. There were several beyond hot guys and girls there, but they were different. They looked human, but they were too gorgeous. Their eyes seemed to glow and they had sharper than normal teeth."

"Was this shortly after your seventeenth birthday?" Grace asked.

"Yeah, it was, as a matter of fact. You don't think I'm crazy?" Lola bit her lower lip nervously.

"I'm going to tell you something you may not want to hear, but I want you to keep an open mind, okay?" Lola nodded her head as Aunt Grace continued, "My grandmother used to tell me all kinds of stories about the Fae. She talked about them as if they were real. She told me our family was blessed and cursed with the gift of Sight. Some of us can see beyond what normal people can see. She said it was a blessing to know the truth of what goes on in the world, but also a curse because people without Sight won't believe it. I didn't understand what she meant until after my seventeenth birthday."

Lola held her breath. Finally, some answers!

Grace kept explaining, "I started seeing these beautiful creatures, some human-like, some not, many of them in the forest, but a few in town. Some of them were unbelievably beautiful from afar.

"I remember one time I was with my friend Lacey and she described this gorgeous guy she had started dating who was supposed to meet us at the diner, but when I saw him, I SAW him. He looked gorgeous from afar, but as he approached, I could see beyond his beauty. His face was all hard edges and points with well-defined cheekbones, a sharp jaw, and a pointed nose, even his ears seemed to come to a point. His eyes were a swirling gold that seemed to glow at times. He smiled at me slowly and when he revealed his teeth, they were sharper than normal human teeth." Grace paused to check on Lola's reaction.

Lola's heart was pounding as she snapped her elastic, thankful for the sting reminding her that this conversation was really happening. "Please keep going," she begged.

Grace took a deep breath. "Well, of course I was totally flustered. How could Lacey not see those differences? I tried to pretend nothing was wrong but later, as she left us to use the restroom, I could see a predatory gleam surfacing in his eyes when he looked at me. I held it together until she returned, keeping up polite conversation though every instinct in me wanted to run. After Lacey and I left her beau and the diner, I told her he'd made a pass at me and was no good so she wouldn't see him again. When I got home, I asked my grandma about it. She told me the Sight was now mine. I didn't want to believe her, but I couldn't ignore what I had seen. She also told me not to let the Fae know I could see through their magic, because they might harm me or try to take me away. I'm sorry, Lola. I should have told you sooner. I just wasn't sure if you would inherit the Sight. It can skip around sometimes. My sister—your grandmother—never received it, but your mother did. It really doesn't surprise me that you did too. Does this have anything to do with your nightmares?"

"Yes," Lola admitted. "At that same party, there was this guy. He had platinum spiky hair and icy blue eyes that seemed to glow." Lola took a deep breath, trying to calm herself before she went on. "I didn't feel well, so I went to find a bathroom and found a bedroom instead. When I turned to leave, the boy was there. He pushed me on to the bed."

Grace gasped and held her hand up to her mouth. Her eyes softened with sympathy. "Oh sweetie…"

"I wasn't—he didn't—" Lola started, but she couldn't bring herself to say what she feared would have happened to her if she hadn't fought. "I think he would have, but I fought—hard. Someone heard me screaming and called 911. They thought I might have…" Lola swallowed, embarrassed to reveal the next part. "They thought I might have taken some bad drugs and was hallucinating, because no one could see the boy when I was fighting to get him off of me. Could he have disappeared or made himself invisible to them?"

"It's possible," Grace answered.

"That's why Dad sent me out here. I had some problems with drugs and they thought it had caused the episode. I went to rehab and therapy, and now I think maybe he was afraid I was becoming like Mom," Lola finished, holding her breath and hoping her admission wouldn't cause Grace to love her less. She looked up at her great-aunt, searching her face for any trace of disappointment, but all she saw was sympathy and love.

"I'm so sorry you had to go through that, Lola," Grace

said softly, her voice full of empathy.

A thought tugged at Lola's memory. "I just remembered—the boy said something really weird. He kept talking about someone being pleased to know I was alive. He made it sound like he was going to take me to someone he worked for." She shivered as she remembered his cryptic words.

"Interesting. I'm not sure who would know about you in the Fae realm. I try to keep an eye and an ear on things, but it's hard. I have a contact on the other side, but most Fae would want to do us both harm if they knew we could see past the glamour they use to look like normal humans. I'll be sure to ask my source when I see her next week. Have you had any other incidents like that one?" Grace inquired.

"Well…" Lola didn't really want to admit what she had come to believe about Conall, but the proof was overwhelming. "Can Fae invade your dreams?"

"Some of them can, yes. They all possess special powers of varying degrees. Some have to do with manipulating the earth, others with human emotions, and some with dreams. I've also heard of Fae who could travel across realms in the blink of an eye, or camouflage themselves completely with their surroundings. You should really try to read some more of your mother's books. They're brimming with useful information," Grace explained.

That affirmed what Lola had come to realize. "I started having dreams about meeting a handsome guy by the tall oak in the clearing. I thought I saw him there a few times, but I wasn't sure if he was real because of my past experiences and what the doctors told me. A few nights I dreamed of meeting him down there and talking to him."

Grace gaspe., "Oh, Lola, you must always be wary of

the Fae. There's so much you don't know. They can be manipulative and cruel to humans. This guy may not be one of the good ones. You see, there are two different factions, or courts, within the Fae: the Seelie and the Unseelie. The Seelie Fae are more likely to have positive interactions with humans. They see their relationships with humans as mutually beneficial, so they don't feel the need to harm them. The Unseelie Fae are more malevolent and gain pleasure from causing pain or chaos. Of course, there are always exceptions to the rule. Not all Seelie Fae like humans and some of them can be malicious, while you may find an occasional Unseelie who respects humans. Most of the time those exceptions will try to keep that part of themselves hidden from the other Fae, because most societies tend to outcast those who don't fit their mold." Lola instantly thought of the way her father seemed to outcast her after she no longer fit his mold. Grace continued, "If he's Unseelie or a Seelie exception, it could mean problems for us. Does he know you can see past his glamour, his human appearance?"

"I don't think so," Lola fibbed. She didn't want to admit that her Spock nickname may have unknowingly given her away.

Aunt Grace released a sigh of relief. "Thank goodness for that. Be careful, dear—he may want something you don't want to give. Be sure to keep your Sight hidden. Tell me about him so I can ask Enora, my contact."

As she told Grace what she knew about Conall, she started to worry. He hadn't seemed like he wanted to cause her harm. In fact, if she remembered correctly, he seemed upset when she didn't trust him, and she hoped Aunt Grace was simply overreacting. She knew in her bones that Conall was good.

CHAPTER 10

TWO NIGHTS LATER as Lola was getting ready for bed, she glanced out the window, searching for Conall out of habit, and there he was, leaning against the tall oak. While she knew she should be cautious, she couldn't help feeling excited about seeing him again. Her aunt was already asleep, so she threw her clothes back on, crept down the stairs, grabbed her boots, and snuck out the door. The clouds hiding the moon made it a little more difficult to see, so she focused on not tripping over her own two feet as she crossed the clearing. When she glanced up, she was by the tall oak, but he had gone.

"Conall?" she called out. The hair on the back of her neck prickled and she fought to shake off the cold chills that swept over her body. "Hey Spock, are you there?" she asked into the darkness of the woods.

She crept past the tree, taking several cautious steps into the woods beyond. With no moonlight and under the cover of trees, it was even harder to see through the darkness. A twig snapped to her right and she spun, expecting to find him, but she only saw shadows. "Conall?" she whispered anxiously. Something didn't feel right about this. She turned to go back to the house then suddenly an arm wrapped around her stomach from behind, holding her firmly in place.

"Hello again, little one," an eerily familiar voice whispered in her ear seductively. She froze in fear and closed her eyes. *This can't be real.*

This can't be real.

"I hope you will be much more cooperative this time." She could feel his warm breath caressing her neck, and her stomach rolled. His tongue snaked out and licked the shell of her ear. She suppressed a revolted shudder and the bile rising in her throat. "Mmmm…too bad we don't have enough time to really enjoy ourselves, but now that my uncle knows you're here, he's expecting you."

Lola worked her hands together and snapped her rubber band against her wrist—unfortunately this was not just a nightmare. It was real. Finally she found the strength to move. "I'm not going anywhere with you," she hissed. "Get your filthy hands off of me." He chuckled and she could feel his chest shake behind her. She started to struggle.

"Now, now, none of that again, or I just may have to hurt you. Actually, on second thought, go right ahead. I think I'd like to hear you cry in pain. Girls always taste so much better with a hint of fear." He tugged her closer.

She struggled harder, but she wasn't getting anywhere. His hands held her in a viselike grip and she wasn't sure she would be able to break free. She took a deep breath, ready to release a scream, but he jerked her around. "If you scream, I'll be forced to cover your mouth"—his tongue snaked out again to lick his own lips in what appeared to be a seductive manner, although it just made her want to vomit—"with my own. If I remember correctly, you do taste quite sweet."

Using the only leverage she had left, she jerked her knee up with as much force as she could manage into the one place she knew could hurt any male. His hands suddenly released her, shoving her backward as he hissed in pain. Lola wasted no time. She scrambled to her feet, feeling twigs digging into her palms, and took off running. She was turned around after his assault and couldn't find the right direction to get to the clearing. The dark forest around her was unfamiliar and she wondered if he had pulled her farther into it without her knowing. She ran as fast as she could, ignoring the small branches that tugged at her clothes and skin. Finally she saw some moonlight breaking through the thick of the woods and prayed it was the clearing. *Smack!* She ran right into a hard, massive body and arms gently grasped hers. Instantly she fought to break free.

"What's wrong, milady?" Conall's voice had never been more musical to her ears, but she noticed a hard edge to it this time. His hands rested on her shoulders firmly, but gently.

She fought to catch her breath. "Someone—after me—wants to kidnap me—attacked me." Conall growled, pivoting around and looking for her attacker.

"Don't worry. I will protect you," he stated, drawing a sword from a sling across his back.

"I must go back to my house. My aunt will worry," Lola pleaded.

"I'm sorry, but we can't go back. He most likely knows where you live, and you are in danger if you stay there,"

Conall argued.

"But, my aunt…" Lola bit her lower lip.

"Don't worry. I'm sure she will be safe since she is not the one he is after," Conall replied. "Come. I don't know if it is wise to stay here any longer. I have somewhere we can go." He took her hand in his free one and pulled her deeper into the woods.

CHAPTER II

LOLA THOUGHT SHE should probably be panicking. There she was with one Fae when another had
just attacked her. Her aunt had told her to be cautious
of Conall, but she felt like she could trust him, and what
other choice did she have? At least if he was evil, he was
the lesser of two evils for the moment. Her feelings warred
inside—safe in his firm grip, but also unsure of his mo-
tives. Where had he been the last two weeks? Why had
he just shown up now? They walked for about an hour in
silence before she needed a break.

"Conall, I need to rest. I wasn't prepared to hike through
the woods all night. Can we stop please?" she begged. He
looked around intently, studying the surrounding forest.

"I think it is safe now," he replied.

She sat down on a fallen tree splayed across the forest
floor to rest her feet. Thank God she had grabbed her boots
and not her flip-flops or they would have been screwed.
"Why would someone be after me?" she asked, hoping he
may have an answer.

He hesitated. "Perhaps he's just crazy." She could tell he wasn't being completely honest with her. "Perhaps he mistook you for someone else. Have you seen this man before?"

"Y-Yes," she stammered. She really didn't want to discuss that again, especially not with him. What would he think of her if he knew the truth? She instead changed topics quickly. "Where are we headed?"

He raised his eyebrow to let her know he wasn't going to let things go with that simple explanation, but decided to answer her question first. "We are going to my home. There are a few things you should know about me first, and after we discuss those, we will talk about the man and when you saw him before."

"Let me guess"—she sighed—"you're going to tell me you're Fae right? Well, I already had that figured out."

His lips parted in surprise. "How did you know?" *Oops*, she thought, having forgotten that no one should know about her Sight.

"Um, I guessed," she answered meekly, but he didn't buy it. "You know what? I'm feeling much better now, thanks. I think we should keep going," she gushed as she hopped to her feet and started jogging away from him in the same direction they'd been heading before.

"Don't think this conversation is over," he called out before he continued walking leisurely after her. It didn't take long for him to catch up to her.

After another hour spent dodging all his questions by ignoring them, she started lagging behind. Exhausted couldn't even begin describe how she felt. It had to be past midnight, and she certainly wasn't used to so much walking. Her boots felt like they were starting to rub her feet raw. What she wouldn't have given for a pair of good trail runners right about then. Conall stopped and waited for her to catch up.

"We are almost there. We will be passing through the gateway into the Fae realm in the next few minutes. You may experience some discomfort. I'm not quite sure how it works for humans. Can you make it for a bit farther?" he asked.

"I guess," she mumbled, still walking at a snail's pace. Sure enough, after a few minutes, he paused. While the woods were still dark, the clouds in front of the moon seemed to have dispersed because she could see her surroundings better. She couldn't help but take in the beautiful sight in front of her. In the moonlight, Conall's muscles looked well defined under the tight, forest green shirt he was wearing, whose color brought out the green in his eyes even more. Several strands of his wavy hair had escaped his ponytail, which she had noticed was bound with a strap of leather. Her fingers itched to tuck one of the strands behind his ear and run across his jaw.

"Did you get your fill?" he asked with a smirk across his handsome face. Her face turned beet red. He had caught her ogling him like a starving dog gazing at a steak. She was surprised she wasn't drooling. Shaking her head to free her mind, she finally noticed what he was standing in front of: two white-barked sycamore trees that stood out from the shadows. They were shorter than the rest of the trees in the forest and two of their branches curved, appearing to reach out toward each other until they met and entwined. It was a beautiful and surreal sight that created the appearance of an archway. She wondered if her Sight allowed her to see it as it truly was. Surely they wouldn't make it so apparent to humans.

"This is the gateway into the Fae realm. Are you ready?" He reached out his hand toward her, and she gratefully grabbed it. The second their skin touched she felt like she was complete, like something she hadn't even known she was missing had found its way back to her. Warmth spread from her fingers down to her toes and she couldn't help the smile that graced her lips. She stepped through the archway of the white sycamores behind him. Her skin tingled from head to toe and she swayed upon her feet for a moment. He instantly turned to steady her, and she stumbled against his chest. He radiated an alluring heat that she didn't want to leave. With her ear that close to his chest, she could hear the subtle way his heart picked up speed and the hitching of his breath. "Are you okay?" he whispered in her ear.

She relished the warmth of his breath against her neck. Realizing she couldn't stay there forever, she quickly regained her composure and took a step back. "Yeah, I'm fine," she said breathlessly. Conall slid his hands up her arms and she closed her eyes at the pleasant sensation. They came to rest on her shoulders and she glanced up into his eyes, which swirled with bright spring green and shimmered in the moonlight. She saw his jaw clench as he swallowed, and she wet her lips. When she looked back, his eyes were staring at her mouth. He seemed to remember himself and cleared his throat, releasing his hands from her at the same time.

"Not much longer now," he said as he turned to lead her forward.

Still feeling slightly dizzy on top of the exhaustion settling into her bones, Lola wasn't sure how much farther she could go. Her boots felt like lead weights dragging her through quicksand. She glanced around at the Fae realm. It looked similar to the woods they had been in before, but the colors were much more vibrant. It was like watching a nature program on regular TV and then suddenly having everything switch into HD. It was breathtaking and beautiful even in the moonlight. She wanted to stop and smell the flowers along the way, but she couldn't find the energy. She wondered where he lived and where she would stay once they got there. At that point she was so exhausted she would have happily slept on a bed of rocks. Her foot caught on a tree root and she tripped, ungracefully sprawling onto the forest floor. "Ow," she groaned.

"Are you okay?" His concern was touching considering she probably would have been bent over laughing if he pulled something as equally clumsy.

"I think I'm just going to rest here for a moment," she muttered, closing her eyes. She was too exhausted to even push herself up. She started drifting off when she felt her body being lifted and cradled against a warm, hard chest. She breathed in deeply, inhaling his unique woodsy scent. She sighed contentedly. She thought she heard a low growl from Conall, but thought she must have been mistaken. She snuggled deeper into his chest, feeling completely safe, and fell asleep.

CHAPTER 12

"WAKE UP, MILADY," Conall whispered against her hair. "We're here." Lola stirred awake and blinked up into his gorgeous green eyes. His awaiting smile was a glorious sight. "Did you enjoy your rest?" he asked, setting her down on her feet.

She instantly missed his warm embrace, but was curious to see where 'here' was. She looked at a small log cabin. It was cozy, blending in with the forest with ivy creeping up the sides. A glowing lantern hung from a post next to the front door. "Well it's not the Shire," she teased, "but it's still cute."

"The Shire?" he puzzled.

"It's a book-slash-movie reference—not important," she replied, too tired to explain. She slipped her hand into his as he tugged her toward the front door. He opened the door and stood back to let her inside first. The interior of his home was sparse but inviting, and everything in the cabin seemed to be there out of function. The front room was a living room, dining room, and small kitchen all in one. There was a couch and chair constructed from tree branches and cushions that looked quite comfortable centered on a rug that appeared to be made out of moss, a small table for two also made of wood, and a small kitchen area with counters, a cooler, a sink, and an old-fashioned stove.

She glanced at Conall. His eyes were glued to her face, studying her expression as she took in his home. He looked like a proud child showing off a work of art, nervously assessing her reaction. "It's rustic and cute. I like it," she praised. He released a breath in a small sigh of relief. *Who knew the big, strong Fae would be nervous about showing a girl his house?* Lola held back the giggle that desperately wanted to escape her lips.

"Please sit while I grab something to tend to your wounds," he requested.

"My wounds?" She looked down. Her arms were covered in small scratches she hadn't noticed before. They must have happened when she was running from her attacker. "Oh," she mumbled. She moved toward the branched chair and sat down. It was heaven to rest her tired bones on something so soft, and she moaned quietly.

Conall returned with a basin of water, a cloth, and a towel. He dipped the cloth in the water and gently took her left arm, cleaning each scratch. Then he moved on to her right arm, giving it equal attention and tending. He was so gentle and focused on her; it warmed Lola's heart. *Is this what it's like to be truly cared for?* she wondered. Next he untied her boots and slipped them off of her feet. Then he started to gently remove her socks and she hissed because it felt like he was tugging some of her skin off. She must have had several blisters pop, and her socks clung to the raw open skin. "I'm sorry. It's going to hurt, but I must tend to them. I will try to make it as quick and painless as possible," he assured her.

She took a deep breath as he pulled the rest of her left sock off. Sure enough, there were several raw blisters. He rolled up her jeans and placed her foot in the warm water. It stung but also felt good at the same time. He did the same with her right foot and slid it into the water. She whimpered as he gently rubbed her ankles and cleaned her blisters. After a few minutes, he pulled her feet out of the water and gently patted them dry with the towel. He got up smoothly with his supplies in hand, took them back to the kitchen, and disappeared into another room. He returned with a tin of some sort of salve. "This will help them heal quickly," he explained. He opened the container and gently rubbed it on each blister and each tiny cut. The salve tingled pleasantly for a few minutes and then felt warm. She wondered what was in it, if it was herbal or Fae magic or a little bit of both, but didn't have much time to consider it as her eyelids drooped.

"Drink first before you rest," he ordered. She opened her eyes to find him in front of her, holding a glass of liquid.

"What is it?" she asked.

"It's good for you," he replied.

She rolled her eyes. "Thanks for that wonderfully descriptive answer, Spock."

He smiled as she lifted the cup to her lips and sipped. It tasted sweet and refreshing, like some sort of fruit juice, but she couldn't name the fruit. She didn't realize how thirsty she was until she had drained the entire cup. "Ahh," she sighed. "Thank you."

"You are safe here, milady. I will protect you. You should rest." He lifted her up and carried her to his small bedroom, where he placed her gently on the bed. "There is a restroom through the other door. I will sleep out in the main room." Lola opened her mouth to protest, but he placed a finger over her lips. "Please do not argue. I insist." She closed her mouth again, savoring the feel of his finger against her lips. He turned to leave the room.

"Conall," she called. "Why do you call me your lady?"

"Milady," he corrected, his cheeks flushing. "It's a term of respect for someone above my station."

"Above your station? What are we? In the Middle Ages? I'm just a regular teenage girl. I'm no one special."

He looked flustered, struggling to answer her question. "You may have forgotten us, but many around here still remember you, Ayanna," he explained.

Lola gasped, no longer feeling tired, but instead, wide awake. She sat up quickly. "How do you know Ayanna?" she demanded, raising her voice in panic. "Who told you about her?" *Why would he know my mother's name?*

Conall furrowed his brow. "Why do you refer to yourself in the third person?"

"I am not Ayanna. My name is Lola—well, my middle name is Lola. Ayanna was my mother."

He tipped his head back as if looking to the heavens—a smile playing at the corners of his lips "You are not Ayanna? Well, that certainly explains some things. I thought perhaps you were using human disguises like hair dye to change your appearance or that perhaps someone had erased your memory. You look a lot like her, you know." His momentary relief was replaced by something darker. He clenched his jaw, leaving her as confused as ever. "Are you by chance wearing contacts?"

She shook her head, her eyes narrowing. "How do you know what my mother looked like?" She repeated her question from earlier, adding, "What do you know about her?"

"I really shouldn't be the one to tell you this, Lola." He said her name like it left a bad taste in his mouth and wrinkled his nose. He paused before continuing, "You said Lola is your middle name—what is your given name?"

Well that was an abrupt shift in the conversation. "You mean my first name?" she asked, and he nodded in response. "It's Ianthe."

"Ianthe…*Ianthe*." This time he said her name like he wanted to savor it. "That is beautiful. I can see why it is your given name—violet flower to match those beautiful violet eyes."

Lola blushed in spite of being annoyed. "Well that's all well and good, Spock, but back to the topic at hand—my mother."

Conall hesitated at first and then breathed out the rest of the sentence in a rush. "Well, you see, Ayanna was once betrothed to my king."

"I'm sorry—did I hear you correctly?" She struggled to process his words. "She was engaged to your king? Your *Fae* king?" *What. The. Hell? Is he serious? There was no way my mother would have been engaged to a Fae.*

"Yes, Ianthe, my *Fae* king. Your mother was betrothed to him. She spent some time here in Fae, living at the castle. She was too kind for him, too tenderhearted, and she vanished around five years ago, although time between the two realms is a funny thing. My guess is that she vanished—" he paused looking her up and down, "around 18 years ago your time. The king would not talk about why she disappeared. The rumor was they had a huge fight and she no longer wished to stay in Fae, so she fled and hid. As a result, I was assigned the duty of watching your great-aunt's house for her return. I did not know I would find you instead. I was confused because you look so much like her when she was here except for the hair and your violet eyes. I should have realized she wasn't you sooner, but I thought maybe someone had tampered with your—her memories." He opened his mouth to say more, but then seemed to think better of it and closed it again.

"I don't believe it. Why would she do that? Aunt Grace told her not to let them know. What was she thinking?" Lola thought aloud. "I can't believe she was engaged to one, let alone the king!"

"Let them know?" Conall inquired quirking his brow. *Damn.* She had slipped again, and she thought maybe she should just come clean. He had been so caring and gentle and sweet; surely it couldn't hurt to tell him about her Sight. How could she get out of this one? She bit her lower lip nervously, trying to think of a response to his question while still processing the shock from the news of her mother's love affair. Her brain was too confused to give her a good excuse.

"I'm feeling very tired. Can we talk about this in the morning?" Hopefully he would accept her answer.

He quirked his eyebrow higher in such an irresistibly cute way, she almost gave in and told him everything. Instead she faked a yawn. He released a sigh of acceptance. "Of course, Ianthe. We *will* discuss it in the morning. Sleep well, my violet flower." His tone let her know he would remember the conversation the next day. He closed the door quietly behind himself as he left the room. Lola's mind spun with all this new information, but her body was so exhausted that she had no time to think before sleep pulled her under.

CHAPTER 13

LOLA WAS RUNNING through the woods. Something was chasing her. Her feet stung and she realized she was barefoot, but it didn't slow her down. She couldn't let him catch her. Twigs stabbed her soles, but she kept pushing forward through the woods. Finally she broke into the clearing. She almost wept with joy at the sight of her aunt's house in the distance. "Aunt Grace, Aunt Grace!" she yelled as she kept running. The grass in the clearing was a soft relief to her feet.

She paused for a moment to catch her breath and glanced over her shoulder. He was at the tree line. He laughed, sending chills down her spine. "Run as far as you want, little one, but you won't escape me."

She turned and sprinted toward the door. She raced up the porch steps and almost tripped on the last one but caught herself just in time. She slammed the door shut and locked it. "Aunt Grace?" she called.

She was bent over, trying to get some air, when she heard his voice outside the house: "Ahh, the chase does make catching the prey ever so sweet." She shuddered and ran toward the kitchen, calling Grace's name. She pushed through the swinging door and froze. There he was in her kitchen, leaning against the island.

"Now, now, I did warn you that you wouldn't escape me," he admonished. His icy blue eyes swirled with malice as he licked his lips. "This time I fully intend to feast upon my prey." He reached for her, his movements inhumanly quick, and grabbed her wrists. She struggled against him, but he pulled her to the side and pushed her against the wall. She could feel his body pressed against hers. The harder she struggled, the more his grip tightened; it felt as if he was going to crush her wrists, and she whimpered. Upon hearing it, he groaned and pressed into her more. Her stomach felt like the spin cycle on a washing machine; she was going to pass out or vomit. She tried to knee him in the groin again, but he had learned from his mistake and kept himself pinned against her too closely. She did the only other thing she could think of. She shifted her weight to her left foot and brought her right foot down on his, stomping as hard as she could.

He grunted. "You are going to pay for that, little one," he ground out through clenched teeth. His grip slackened, but not enough. Instead he pulled her violently toward him and bit her shoulder. She screamed as pain ripped through her. She could feel the blood trickling down her arm, warm and wet. He pulled his head back, lips red with her blood, and licked them. "Mmmm...you taste even sweeter from the chase."

She heard her name called in the distance, over and over again: "Ianthe! Ianthe!" She fought to hold back tears, not wanting to give the monster in front of her the satisfaction of seeing them fall. He growled and shook her shoulders.

She blinked her eyes open with a gasp. Conall was leaning over her, shaking her gently. "Ianthe." He breathed a sigh of relief. Tears instantly sprang to her eyes and she started to tremble and cry. She couldn't hold it in any longer. That nightmare had been so much worse than the last one. She was afraid of blue-eyed boy, afraid he would find her eventually since he already had once before. Would she ever be safe from him? Fear turned her trembling into full-on shaking.

Conall held her while she sobbed and tried to soothe her, running a comforting hand through her hair. "It's okay, my flower. I'm here now. No one will hurt you," he repeated over and over again in her ear. It took her quite some time to regain control. Her tremors slowed, and soon after, so did her sobbing. She sniffed and looked up at him with watery, bloodshot eyes.

"Thank you," she whispered.

"There's no need to thank me. I only wish I could have woken you sooner. I heard you scream and came as soon as I could. I tried calling your name, but you would not wake. Are you okay?" His concern was genuine and warmed her heart, chasing away the last bit of ebbing fear. His hand stroked her hair and came to rest against her face.

She leaned into his palm and took a deep breath. "Yes, I think I'm okay now. Thank you for waking me. I had a nightmare, and he was there. He was chasing me again."

"Who was?" Conall pressed. "The man who chased you last night?"

"Yes," she huffed. She really didn't want to bring him back up. The mere thought of him sent her stomach rolling and started to make her hands tremble.

He caught on to her sudden shift. "It's okay. You don't have to tell me now. I just hope you feel up to telling me later when it does not cause you such distress."

"Thank you, Conall," Lola whispered. She looked into his eyes, trying to tell him she wasn't just thanking him for dropping the subject but also for rescuing her the previous night, for waking her from her nightmare, for everything.

Conall smiled and stroked his strong hand down her hair once more. He caught a lock around his fingers and glanced down. "I think I rather like the blue. It's growing on me." The corner of his mouth tugged up into a crooked smile that warmed Lola from head to toe. "Since we're both up now, why don't I make us something to eat?" he said, standing up and tugging Lola's hand, and she followed him out of the room.

Chapter 14

AFTER A QUIET breakfast of polite conversation, Lola decided to bring up something that had been bothering her since she'd realized Conall was Fae. She was pretty sure she had figured it out, but she wanted to hear it from him to reassure herself. "Conall," she started, "can I ask you something?"

"But of course, Ianthe. Ask away," he replied. She ducked her head, hiding her eye roll at his blatant refusal to call her Lola.

She took a deep breath. "Are you Seelie or Unseelie Fae?" she whispered hesitantly. Her heart hammered in her chest, waiting for his reply. She needed him to say Seelie like she needed air to breathe. She wanted to believe he was good and didn't want to harm her. She risked a glance at his face, scanning his features for his reaction.

He grimaced, and in response, her heart picked up speed. He licked his lips nervously, and she felt as if her heart would break through her ribcage. "How do you know so much about Fae?" he asked.

Well, that wasn't the response I was looking for. In fact, it wasn't an answer to her question at all. She frowned but held her ground. "Conall, I need you to answer my question first." She was amazed that her voice sounded steady and didn't waver, reflecting her inner turmoil.

"Ianthe—" he started, but then he was interrupted by loud banging on his front door that made him jump from his seat, his face stricken with panic. He grabbed Lola's hand. "I am not expecting company. Please go into my room as quietly as you can and close the door. Stay quiet until I come get you. Do you understand?" he whispered anxiously, hurriedly pulling her from the couch.

Lola nodded fearfully, crept as quietly as she could into the room, and closed the door behind her. She heard the front door open and him speaking to someone. She pressed her ear against the door as a deeper voice replied. Footsteps approached the main room and started pacing. Lola silently cracked the door, anxious to hear more. "Did you find her?" the deeper voice asked. Lola gasped. *Are they talking about me?*

"Yes, sir…but there were some, um, complications." Conall hesitated, gathering his thoughts.

"Complications? What kind of complications? I would not trust this task to anyone but my first in command, Conall. Do not disappoint me," the other male replied, his voice rising into a growling yell.

"She's not who you think she is, sir. She's not Ayanna," Conall explained. Lola's breath caught in her throat and her palms started to sweat. She swallowed despite the sudden dryness that had overtaken her mouth and inched the door open farther while still staying hidden.

"Then who is she?" the other man demanded.

Conall's voice dropped to a whisper, but Lola still

caught it. "She's Ayanna's daughter."

The man inhaled sharply, obviously not expecting that twist. "Her…her daughter?" he stammered incredulously. "B-But…but that just can't be."

"I'm sorry, my lord, but it is the truth. She looks just like Ayanna, but she's too young…and there are other differences too," Conall continued. Lola's mind caught on to two words: *my lord*. The pieces started clicking into place. *Conall is this man's first in command. The only person he would call my lord is the king—the Fae king who was engaged to my mom!* Lola's balance waivered and her knees shook. She reached down and snapped her elastic against her wrist, causing a small sting. It wasn't enough. She couldn't believe what was happening just outside the door. She pulled the elastic back farther and released. It resonated loudly and an involuntary cry escaped her lips at the sting.

"What was that?" the Fae king demanded. "Who's there?" he called out. She heard heavy footsteps approach the door, and she scrambled backward to hide from view. The door was shoved open just as she ducked behind the bed. "I know you're in here," he growled. "Conall! I demand to know who is here with you right now."

Lola peeked under the bed as Conall's boots approached the doorway. "I apologize, Your Majesty. I should have said something sooner and was hoping to explain. Ianthe, would you come out please? It's okay. No one will hurt you," Conall called.

Slowly Lola raised herself out of her crouch behind the bed. She saw Conall's muscular legs standing in the doorway but focused on the other pair of legs off to the left. His clothes reminded her of rich kings from the past— tall, black leather riding boots over black pants. Her eyes traveled up the Fae king's body as she rose to her feet. Over the black pants, he was wearing a belted violet tunic made of silk. He had several large gold rings on his fingers. Her eyes traveled farther, and she took in his broad shoulders. She titled her head up to see his face and gasped in surprise. He had shoulder-length hair that shimmered and appeared to be a shade between pearl and silver, his face young with a somewhat familiar curve to his chin, but that wasn't what made her gasp. It was his eyes. They were the exact same shade of violet as her own.

She heard his sharp intake of breath and found the man's eyes studying her as well. "Conall, how can this be?" he whispered.

Conall chuckled from the doorway, but Lola couldn't draw her eyes away from the Fae king to see what was so funny. "Why, my lord, I think you would be better able to answer that than myself." She caught a hint of amusement to Conall's response, but her mind was spinning. *So this is the Fae king—the same Fae king my mother was with. Why does he have my eyes?*

She covered her mouth as the epiphany hit her.

He doesn't have my eyes—I have his.

"No, no, no. This can't be possible. No, it just can't be. I know my father, and this is not him," she whispered, trying to convince herself more than anyone else. She glanced at the Fae king's face. His eyes had softened and the shock she had seen earlier was now replaced with awe.

She traced her right hand down her left, toward her rubber band. She had to be dreaming. This could not possibly be happening; it was just too surreal. As she reached the elastic and pulled it back, she suddenly felt Conall's hand over her own, holding the rubber band back against her wrist. "Ianthe, you know I don't like that," he stated, daring her to try again.

The Fae king cleared his throat loudly. "Conall, when did you know?" he asked.

"I wasn't sure until just now, sir," Conall replied as he released Lola's wrist and stepped back, dropping his sharp gaze from Lola's eyes.

"I'm sorry—Ianthe, is it?" the Fae king interrupted, stepping into her space. His eyes narrowed as he gave her a closer inspection. "Could you please tell me your age?"

Lola licked her lips and turned her attention toward him. "Actually, it's Lola, sir, and I, um, I just turned seventeen a few months ago." She swallowed, feeling the nerves building in her system. She didn't want to hear him say it. It would ruin everything she knew. It would mean her father wasn't her father and her mother was a stranger. She would no longer know what she was and where she came from. It was too much to process. She studied his face and could almost see him working through the math in his head. Before he could say anything, she jumped in, hoping to delay his response. "Um, I'm sorry, but who are you?" she asked.

He raised his eyebrow and released a small breath. "Of course, my apologies, we have not been properly introduced. I am Corydon, the Unseelie king." She felt as if the wind had been knocked out of her. She stared at her feet. Her mother had been involved with not just a Fae king, but the Unseelie king! She couldn't breathe. *This can't be happening.*

"Lola," she heard Lord Corydon say.

"Ianthe," Conall called, but she couldn't answer any of them because she couldn't breathe as the panic settled in. She gasped for breath as her lungs began to burn, craving the oxygen she couldn't provide. Suddenly she felt strong hands gently grab her face until she was staring straight into swirling, bright green eyes. "Breathe, Ianthe," Conall whispered. She felt herself calming from his touch and sucked in a deep breath, oxygen filling her lungs and dissipating the burn inside her. "Now breathe out," he commanded, keeping his hands against her cheeks, framing her face, his eyes glued to hers. She released her breath slowly and found she could breathe normally once again.

"Thank you." She sighed, instantly disheartened when he pulled his hands away from her face. He glanced over his shoulder at his king and seemed embarrassed. *Is he embarrassed by me? Wait, if Conall's king is the Unseelie king that means—* "You're Unseelie too," Lola accused, looking at Conall.

His lips formed a tight line. "That is correct," he acknowledged.

Corydon's voice interrupted their little moment, startling her from her thoughts. "Lola, I can't tell you how pleased I am to meet you, I only wish we could have done this sooner." His tone was rigid and held a hint of iciness that she wasn't expecting. It was almost as if he had raised a shield and was now taking an extremely formal approach to her instead of the awe he had looked at her with when he first saw her. Lola still wasn't sure how her mother could have loved him unless she'd been taken in by his beauty, which far surpassed that of anyone she had ever met— well, with the exception of Conall, of course. "Ayanna was an exquisite creature when I knew her, full of beauty and promise. I was rather dismayed when she chose not to stay in the Fae realm with me. I have always searched for her, hoping one day to be reunited." Lola thought she saw a flicker of untamed rage in his eyes, but it was gone in an instant. "Tell me, where is she now?"

"Oh, um…" Lola wasn't sure how to explain it at all.

"She died when I was younger," she said quietly. She studied his face for his reaction. For a moment he looked absolutely devastated, but within a few beats, the shield of formality and indifference slammed into place again, altering his features.

"How unfortunate," he commented, glancing down at his fingernail and scratching at some imaginary mark. "Well, since you are here and we have much to discuss, would you do me the honor of joining me for lunch at the palace?"

She didn't really want to go, but she did have questions, and she wasn't quite sure how the Unseelie king would take being turned down. "I suppose so, if Conall can escort me," she replied, hoping he would be able to join her. She wouldn't feel comfortable walking into the lion's den alone.

"But of course. My first in command is always welcome in my home." Corydon nodded at Conall, who returned the nod. "I will see you both in an hour." He turned abruptly and marched out of the cottage, closing the front door behind him.

Lola wasn't sure what had just happened. She felt so confused and lost. The shock of their meeting faded as an uncomfortable thought tugged at her mind. She didn't know who to trust or what to believe in this strange land, but she had to know the truth. "Conall, why are King Corydon's eyes the same color as mine?" Her heart felt like it skipped a few beats waiting for his response.

Even though Lola and her father had problems, he was still her father. He hadn't always been the distant and hard-to-please man he had become. She remembered how loving and doting he had been when her mother was alive, how every Sunday he would get up before anyone else to cook breakfast for them, how he used to check her closet for monsters. Of course, those memories were few and from such a long time ago, but still.

After what seemed like an eternity, Conall finally responded. "Do you really want me to answer that question?" *Man, he is perceptive.* She shakily nodded her head, hoping his words would not confirm what she now feared. "Well, it is my belief and now King Corydon's belief that you are his…his daughter."

The words hit her like a ton of bricks and knocked the wind out of her.

"The timeline matches with when Ayanna was here, and you do have his eyes. I've only seen that shade of violet run in royal families," Conall continued. There were several minutes of silence following the words that shattered Lola's world. *So if Corydon is my father, does that mean I am part Fae?* "Ianthe, please say something."

She licked her dry lips and opened her mouth several times, but couldn't find any words. *What just happened?* She'd always thought her dad's distance was because she reminded him so much of her mom, but what if it had been something else? What if he somehow knew? She remembered back to when she had asked him about her unique eye color and he replied vaguely that it must be some relative of her mother's that she inherited them from. He'd shrugged off the question and quickly changed topics, as he always did when conversation led to her mother. "Why am I even believing this for a second? I can't be his—I just can't." She started ranting like a madwoman, pacing around the main room. She threw her arms up and tilted her head toward the ceiling, raising her voice. "My mother would never be with a Fae, or a Fae king, but especially not the Unseelie king!" She finally let loose a growling yell of frustration.

Conall looked as if he had been slapped. Pain marked every feature of his face until it hardened and he narrowed his eyes at Lola. "What's so wrong with being Fae, Lola? I'm Fae, or have you forgotten?" he spat. She hadn't thought about how her words would affect him. "If you don't like Fae, you can leave. Go back to your home, Lola. See who will help you then." He turned his back to her and started walking toward the door. She hadn't realized how much she enjoyed him calling her Ianthe until he started calling her Lola.

"Wait! Conall! Please, I'm—I'm sorry. Don't leave," she begged. He paused in the doorway for a moment before shaking his head slightly and stepping outside. The slam of the front door behind him echoed in the main room. "What have I done?" She sighed, slumping onto the couch. How had a day that started so pleasantly ended up in ruin? Hopefully he wouldn't be gone long because she had absolutely no idea where she was and they were expected at the king's place in less than an hour. More importantly, she also had no clue how to get back to her aunt's house—to her home.

CHAPTER 15

CONALL RETURNED FIFTEEN minutes later, although it felt like hours to Lola. She had been lying on the couch trying to sort through the shit storm her life had become when she heard the door open. She sat up quickly. "Conall, I'm so sorry. I didn't mean it—well, not all of it. I was just so upset. I mean, I had just found out that everything I knew about my family—my mother and father—was a lie," she explained. She looked at Conall as he stared at the floor.

"It's fine, Lola," he replied, brushing her off quickly. "We need to get going if we're going to make it to lunch with His Majesty."

She sighed and lifted herself off of the couch. She wished she could swallow back her words, take back the whole conversation and just have it as an inner monologue. She trudged toward the door after him and stepped outside.

She had yet to see the Fae realm in the daylight, and it was like stepping into the most beautiful painting she had ever seen. The sky was an electric, clear blue with not a cloud in sight. The flowers were so vibrant and filled the air with a sweet aroma. The grass and trees were as green as her aunt's clearing after a summer rain, and the whole world looked refreshed. The temperature was pleasant, not too hot and not too cold. She longed to paint it even though she wasn't an artist, and she could understand some of the stories she read about humans wanting to stay in Fae, finding their muse in its beauty. Even the small dirt road on which they were walking was like stepping back in time. She could imagine horse-drawn carts had probably passed through there, and she stumbled on a rock while she was busy taking in the scenery. Instantly Conall spun around and his arms steadied her as if it were a reflex. She was hoping her apology had smoothed things over. "Be careful where you step. Pay more attention," he snapped, quickly releasing her as if she were poisonous. Apparently her apology hadn't been enough.

Before he could march off, she snatched his hand and tugged. "Conall, look, I really am sorry. I didn't think about how my words might affect you." She studied his face for any sign that her apology had been accepted. Unfortunately it was a mask of hardened features.

"Your words did nothing. Do not place so much value on them. Besides, I'm an Unseelie Fae so it shouldn't matter, right?" he seethed. There was the truth, and boy did it sting. She grimaced. *Fine, two can play this game.* She threw his hand down and stomped down the dirt road they were following. *He is so infuriating!* She had apologized, so now it was up to him if he wanted to accept.

They walked in silence for about twenty minutes, both stewing in their own thoughts when she noticed a town in the distance. It looked like a medieval village made of small houses. Dominating the town was a large stone castle like something out of her history textbook. As she walked, she couldn't seem to keep her eyes from darting over toward Conall. She blamed her hormones—he was a fine specimen of the male species. As they approached the castle, she noticed that he seemed to grow nervous and fidgety. She kept walking then felt a warm, strong tug on her hand. Conall had stopped behind her and was tugging her back toward him. She was still angry with him, but she couldn't help the butterflies that rioted in her stomach and the warmth that spread to her toes from the touch of his hand and the sight of his soft gaze. "Ianthe, there's something you need to know." She almost had him stop right there and repeat her name again. She had missed the sound of it coming from his lips. He continued, "The Unseelie Fae are not like me."

She scrunched her brow. "What do you mean?"

He paused and licked his lips, her eyes hungrily tracking every movement of his tongue. His finger tipped her head up so she was looking him in the eyes again. "Ianthe." His voice was low and raspy. *Sweet baby Jesus.* If he spoke her name like that one more time, she would be putty in his hands. She fought to refocus her attention on his words and not his mouth. "What do you know of the Unseelie?"

"I've heard they are malicious and get pleasure from tormenting humans," she stated. She didn't want to give away her source for fear of Aunt Grace's safety.

Conall appeared tortured for a minute then resigned as he released his breath. "That is true of most Unseelie."

"But that's not you, right?"

He swallowed. "Well, I seem to be a unique case. I was born part Unseelie Fae, like you." Lola's stomach turned over at the reminder that she was not fully human. "My father was human and my mother is a succubus. While some full-blooded Fae look down on us half-breeds, I found it gave me a special perspective on humanity. I discovered early on that my instincts were not to use humans, but to help them. This is a very untraditional view from the rest of the Unseelie. Your words upset me earlier because the truth is, we are born Seelie or Unseelie—we don't choose. I can't change the fact that I am Unseelie, just as you can't change the color of your skin," Conall explained.

She felt the urge to come back with a comment about self-tanner but resisted, absorbing the information he was giving her. Conall being part Fae and part human certainly explained why he didn't have the characteristic sharp teeth she had seen on other Fae. "So, your parents are…" she prompted, hoping he would fill in the blank.

"They are both dead to me," Conall stated. "My father died of old age some time ago, and while my mother is still alive, she does not share the same views as I do and chose to disown me many years ago. She doesn't know how to care for anyone other than herself. She views many of the human emotions as weaknesses. She feasts on all the emotions from humans and manipulates them into feeling pleasure or pain or both, but she couldn't care less about them when she is done and tends to dispose of them like trash. I guess I should be lucky she waited to dispose of me until I was old enough to care for myself."

"Oh, Conall. That's so sad," Lola commiserated. She could completely relate to feeling unloved and unwanted by the one parent you had left.

"That's the life of an Unseelie. You will find no warmth in this place. You must always be on your guard. Many of the Fae you will meet would like to eat you for lunch or play with you like a shiny new toy until you break. They are not like me. They view humans as property or prey," he explained. She shivered, bits of her nightmare flashing through her mind. She knew how it felt to be prey and had no desire to repeat that experience. "Do not go anywhere without myself or your father present. I will protect you, and I don't think he will let any harm come to you while you are there."

"You don't *think*?" she asked, stunned by this last piece of information.

Conall looked as if he would rather be swallowing nails than having this conversation with her. "Your father is the Unseelie king, Ianthe. He is a very strong dictator and keeps the Unseelie Fae under control, but he is not known for his kindness. He shows no mercy to those around him, especially if he feels they have betrayed him in some way. I had once hoped he would be a better king than his father before him, but after your mother ran away, he shut off any emotion he had and let the darkness consume him. While you are his daughter, you are also a reminder of his failure to keep your mother happy, and you are half human. It's been harder to work for him as I've seen his contempt for humans increase each year. Please do not repeat anything I have just told you, as some may consider it treason to speak against our king and would be quick to turn me in. Promise me you will always keep your guard up." She felt sick at the idea that her father was the Unseelie king, but as much as she didn't want to believe it, the evidence was piling up.

She took a deep breath to calm her nerves and resisted snapping her elastic because she knew it would only upset him further. "Okay, Conall. I promise. Thank you for warning me." He turned to continue walking toward the houses. "If King Corydon is as you say he is, why are you his first in command?" Lola wondered.

"You don't tell the Unseelie king no and live to tell the tale. I started as one of his guards when he was just a prince. After he took his new position, he wanted me for his first in command, so I accepted. All in all, I've worked for him for over twenty years."

"*Twenty* years? How old are you?" Lola was shocked. He looked to be only about twenty.

"You will find that time passes differently here in the Fae realm. In Fae years I am almost forty-two, which is still quite young, although most Fae stop aging when they turn twenty-five until they reach their first century. We generally live for hundreds of years. As a half-breed, I'm not expected to live as long as, say, the king, but my lifespan and your own should still be rather lengthy if spent in the Fae realm. Also, I was recruited rather young to train for the Unseelie Guard. I think it was because my mother was willing to give me away to anyone who would take me and I was a very strong boy. I was trained by the best and quickly surpassed my instructors. The king sought me for his first in command despite my young age for I am unmatched in my fighting skills. I have speed I inherited from my maternal grandparents, as well as certain incubus aspects that help with negotiations," Conall replied.

"Incubus aspects?" she pried.

"Yes, there are many different kinds of Fae. I happen to be an incubus. Most of our abilities are hereditary—incubuses are generally male and born to a succubus. As an incubus, I can manipulate emotions, both human and Fae alike." He looked at her guiltily.

"Have you ever used your powers on me?" Shame filled his eyes, giving him away instantly. "You did, didn't you? Is that why I always feel so calm when you touch me?"

Conall licked his lips nervously. "Yes, I can calm fear along with influencing many other emotions. I only used it on you because I didn't want you to be afraid of me."

"Let me get this straight: you didn't want me to be afraid of you, so you didn't give me the chance?" She felt anger simmering inside her, turning into a slow boil. "Instead of letting me figure out that you're a great guy, you didn't give me the choice—you took it away. How much of what I've been feeling around you actually belongs to me, Conall?" Her voice rose with each word as her fury boiled over. How could she trust anything she felt when she touched him? Had he been manipulating her the whole time? Had it all been a trick to get her there to meet the king? "I can't believe it!" she snarled, stomping toward the town and trying to get rid of the infuriatingly handsome Fae next to her.

"Ianthe, wait. Let me explain, please," he begged.

"Oh, because you were so eager to hear my explanation earlier. *Right*." She scoffed over her shoulder and picked up her pace. She didn't want to be near him right then. She didn't know what was true and what was lies in that Fae realm, and more than ever, she craved a hug from Aunt Grace. She wished she were sitting back in Aunt Grace's kitchen helping her cook or watching *Supernatural* with her. She wished she had never met Conall at the edge of the clearing and discovered the existence of Fae.

CHAPTER 16

ONALL GAVE HER the space she craved and stayed a few paces behind her while she stomped toward the first of the houses. Remembering his words, he decided to slow her pace as to not appear more like prey. She shuddered, a bit of her nightmare resurfacing: *"The chase does make catching the prey ever so sweet."* She walked calmly through the town, taking in the sights. The houses were a variation of quaint and extravagant medieval, stone-walled cottages with thatched roofs. It almost made her feel like she had stepped back in time, and she swore if the houses were in a hillside, she would be at the Shire. Instead of hobbits she saw Fae with their intense good looks, sharp angular features, pointed ears, and seemingly glowing eyes in a myriad of colors to match the variety of hair colors and skin tones. They seemed surprised to see her there and more than once she heard the name "Ayanna" whispered as she passed. Some looked at her especially predatorily, and she shivered in spite of her attempts at controlling her fear. She instinctively brushed her right hand toward her left wrist to snap her elastic.

"I wouldn't do that if I were you," Conall warned behind her left ear. She could feel his breath on the back of her neck and a calming warmth radiating from his body. How had he caught up to her so quickly? Had he been there all along and she just didn't notice? Before she could blink, he reached over and slid her rubber band off of her wrist. Her eyes went wide; it felt as if someone had taken her beloved safety blanket from her. "Control it, Ianthe," he rumbled. "Some of them can smell fear. Others enjoy pain, and when it is self-inflicted, it draws them even closer."

She slowly drew in a deep breath to soothe her nerves. She resisted the urge to lean into his warmth and absorb some of his calm. She needed to make sure everything she felt was her own, to make sure she was in control of at least one part of her situation. Glancing around, she felt like a gazelle surrounded by a pride of lions, nervous and skittish, just waiting for them to pounce. Slowly she tried to quiet her emotions without her crutch, and while it took some time, eventually she did. She was so focused on controlling her breathing and not freaking out that they had passed through most of the town before she knew it and were now entering the courtyard of the large, grey castle. It reminded her of Castle Ward in Northern Ireland, which was used in *Game of Thrones* for Winterfell. She remembered looking it up later to see if it were a real place and adding it to her bucket list.

Conall leaned in to whisper into her ear again. "Ianthe, remember what I told you earlier. When we go in there, I am not your friend—I am the king's first in command. Regardless, I will do what I can to make sure you are safe," he assured her before stepping away, putting a polite amount of space between them. *Well, there went the only support system I had left—although, what did I expect? Him to suddenly side with me over his own people, over the king he has been serving for decades?* Maybe she didn't expect it, but she certainly wanted it.

Lola paused, glancing at the guards. Both were incredibly handsome with the characteristic pointed features. One had sapphire blue eyes and the other eyes of swirling red. They were dressed in pieces of traditional armor and leather that reminded her of Thor, regal but deadly. She tried to raise her chin and look proud and defiant instead of the scared little girl she was inside. The heavy wooden doors creaked open as she stepped into a great hall.

"Introducing Lady Ianthe and Sir Conall," a voice boomed to her left, catching her off guard. An older woman rushed forward to greet them, but Lola didn't see the king anywhere. The woman was average height and rather round, almost like the blue fairy godmother from *Sleeping Beauty*, middle-aged with black hair pulled back into a severe bun. She stared at Lola with a disapproving glare.

"This will not do—this will not do at all," she admonished, clucking her tongue and surveying Lola at the same time.

Lola glanced at Conall, who had a smirk on his face. "What seems to be the problem, Alvina?" he asked the woman with a hint of amusement.

"She cannot dine with the king looking like *that*," Alvina stated.

"What's wrong with how I look?" Lola asked, even though she knew she was not exactly in her best attire. She had faint pink lines marking her arms where her bloody scratches had been the previous day, her jeans were ripped from her tumble, and God only knew what her hair looked like—she could only hope it wasn't an enormous rat's nest. She didn't attempt to smell herself, but she was sure it wasn't the sweetest scent as she hadn't showered since the other day at her aunt's house and had been running through the woods since. The more she thought about her appearance, the pinker her cheeks grew. She hadn't even thought about the fact that she'd looked that way in front of Conall all day. The embarrassment started sinking in. *Maybe it wouldn't be so bad to freshen up a bit.*

"Well, first of all, you reek of human, not to mention that ladies should not be seen in such frumpy attire. You are Fae, girl, and you need to look and act like it. Follow me, and I will help you get cleaned up." Alvina left no room for argument. Lola glanced at Conall, who shrugged his shoulders and quirked his adorable eyebrow. He followed behind her casually as they climbed the stairs from the great hall.

"Here we are," Alvina announced, stepping toward the third doorway on the left. "Conall, you must wait outside, unless you'd like to join the king in the dining hall." She took one look at Conall's large frame with his arms folded across his chest that clearly stated he wasn't going anywhere. "Suit yourself," she added, stepping through the door and waiting for Lola to enter before closing the door gently behind her. Lola's jaw dropped slightly at the gorgeous room. Every luxury and comfort she could ever imagine was there—a queen-sized pillow-top bed with a canopy, an antique dresser and vanity, and a large mahogany armoire. Several vases of orchids sat throughout the room. It looked feminine and rich, like a super expensive antique hotel room.

"Don't worry, the men will wait for you before dining. First we must get you clean." Alvina wrinkled her nose in Lola's direction, showing some disgust at her appearance.

She led her into the largest bathroom Lola had ever seen. It was probably the size of her bedroom back home. Set into the center of the ivory marble floor was a small pool full of water topped with bubbles and rose petals. If there was one aspect of her life that she always enjoyed indulging in, it was pampering herself.

Alvina excused herself after showing Lola all the soaps and waited for her back in the bedroom. Lola instantly stripped her clothes and stepped into the pool, submerging herself in the soothing water. She sighed as the heat of the bath relaxed her muscles and studied her arms and feet as she washed, noticing that only pink lines or spots showed where her wounds had been the night before. *That salve works wonders.* She scrubbed her hair and body until she felt clean, enjoying the floral scents of the soaps. It was hard to believe she'd been at her aunt's house just the day before. It seemed like ages ago. She guessed running and hiking through the forest in the middle of the night probably had something to do with it, but more so all the change that had barged into her life.

She didn't stay in the bath long; she hated the idea of being without Conall's comforting presence. She wondered if he was still outside her room or if he had joined King Corydon already. She stepped out of the bath and wrapped herself in a white plush towel. Alvina must have heard her because she suddenly appeared at the door. "Come, King Corydon has clothes for you."

Lola's lips parted in surprise and her jaw almost hit the floor when she saw the gown Alvin had selected. It was a deep emerald green that reminded her of Conall's eyes when they darkened. Alvina helped her get into the dress and laced up the bodice in the back. The skirt clung to her hips then flowed out, and it felt softer than silk. Two lace shoulder straps framed her chest in a most appealing manner. Alvina held a pair of heels up next, but Lola definitely didn't want to go there. "Um…I don't wear heels anymore," she declared.

Alvina snorted. "Well, you certainly can't wear those boots with this dress." She pointed an accusatory finger at the offending boots by the doorway.

"Are there any sandals, perhaps?" Lola inquired, willing to compromise.

Alvina dug through the armoire and pulled out a pair of gold Greek lace-up sandals. The thick straps were made of leather, but felt smooth as butter against her skin when Alvina laced them up. Her feet rejoiced at the softness of the shoes. "Now we must do something with your hair. Is that your natural color?" Alvina asked, plucking a blue lock with her fingers.

"No, but I like it. I don't want to change it back," Lola stated. Alvina sighed and shook her head but agreed, gently pushing Lola to sit on the chair she had turned to face away from the vanity. Then she started humming a beautiful tune that almost sounded like angels signing, and while she hummed, she combed her fingers through Lola's hair.

"There. Now hold still," she ordered. She took out what appeared to be a makeup brush and continued her wondrous humming while running the brush across Lola's face. "Done. Take a look," she said, sweeping her arm to the vanity mirror. She looked pleased with herself and Lola was anxious to see why. She stood up from the chair and stepped in front of the mirror and gasped. She looked more beautiful than she had at prom the previous year. Her brown and blue tresses lay in perfect curling waves, not a hair out of place or any of the frizz she usually had to deal with. Her skin had a natural glow that was brought out by the makeup on her face. It looked natural, except her eyes, which were lined with a charcoal grey to enhance their violet color…eyes that shimmered and glowed like those of the Fae in the village, reminding her that she wasn't fully human. *Did Alvina do all this simply by swiping a brush across my face? Maybe it's part of her Fae abilities.*

"Wow. Thank you Alvina," Lola praised.

"No need to thank me," she replied stiffly. "I'm just pleased I could make you look presentable for His Majesty. I don't know why he insists on humans when Fae are so superior. Even a half-breed like yourself should make an effort to look better." Alvina's voice was so condescending and nonchalant that Lola surmised this would probably be the attitude of most Fae, as Conall had warned her. She supposed she must be slightly spoiled having met him first and experiencing his attentive kindness. Without delay, Alvina opened the door and almost plowed right into Conall. He was exactly where Lola had last seen him before her transformation. "Excuse me," Alvina said rudely as she elbowed her way around.

Conall glanced into the doorway at Lola. She had always wondered if she would ever have a movie magic moment, and this was definitely it. His stared at her and his eyes swirled a deep emerald green, matching her dress. He licked his lips as he scanned her from her from bottom to top, his gaze pausing in certain areas that made her heart race. "You look gorgeous, my flower," he rasped in a husky voice that made her insides melt. "Shall we?" he asked, sweeping his arm toward the hall.

CHAPTER 17

LOLA FOLLOWED CONALL back down the stairs and into an opulent dining room. Corydon was relaxing on an ornate golden throne set on a dais. "Wonderful. Now you look more like a Fae princess should," the Unseelie king stated.

"Fae princess?" Lola stammered.

"But of course. If you are my daughter—and I believe you are—then you are most definitely the true heir to the Unseelie throne," he explained. This bit of information did not sit well with her, and she suddenly lost her appetite. She tried to mask her disgust so as not to offend the king, but with a glance at Conall, she knew she wasn't doing a very good job. He shook his head ever so slightly in warning, so she made sure to school her features into a mixture of surprise and joy.

"I used to dream about being a princess," she gushed, practically giggling. Conall quirked his adorable eyebrow at that comment. *Okay, maybe that's laying it on a little too thick.*

"Shall we eat?" King Corydon asked, motioning to a large cherry wood table that had stood empty moments before but was now amazingly filled with all kinds of food. The sudden appearance of the delicious but strange foods reminded Lola of the feast scene in the Great Hall in *Harry Potter and the Sorcerer's Stone*. She reached toward her wrist to snap her elastic, a reminder that yes, this was really happening, but she only encountered skin. Frowning, she remembered Conall had taken it from her. She flicked her eyes up toward him and saw him trying to hide a smile. She narrowed her eyes in return, an unsuccessful attempt at a glare that only seemed to make him smirk more. King Corydon—she refused to think of him as her father—sat at the head of the table. Conall sat on the right side, which left her to take the left.

A servant stepped forward from the corner of the room to serve them. Lola felt uncomfortable with the idea of being waited on while the king completely ignored the servants and Conall acted as if this was daily life, and perhaps to them it was. The food tasted great, but the conversation felt awkward and strained. Several times, the king solely addressed Conall, as if he had forgotten Lola was even in the room. Lola was bored but tried to pay attention to their conversation in case she could learn anything about the Unseelie or Fae in general. She was starting to zone out when King Corydon's voice interrupted her thoughts. "So what do you think, Lola?"

Oh crud. She had missed something, and by the frown on Conall's face, it was something important. The king was looking at her expectantly. "I-I'm sorry, could you repeat that?" she stammered.

"Huh, just like her mother I see," he muttered bitterly before answering her question. "I said I would be most honored if you would stay and spend some time at the palace. I'm sure you have many questions for me and know nothing of your Fae heritage. I'd like to remedy that." His face showed he was not pleased their meeting was the first time she learned she was part Fae.

Lola was about to decline when she remembered Conall telling her no one told the Unseelie king no. "What about Aunt Grace? She'll be worried if I disappear. She's probably already called the police."

"I have sent word to her that you are being well cared for," Corydon stated, as if that would solve all her problems. "If I need to speak with her in person, I can."

Yikes! That would not be good. She quickly jumped in. "No, no. I'm sure the note or however you contacted her is just fine." She sure hoped it would be enough, but somehow she knew her aunt would probably worry even more knowing she was with the Unseelie king, and that didn't sit well with her. She tried not to let her panic show. She stared at her hands in her lap, aching for her missing elastic band, and smoothed down her dress. "Spending some time here would be lovely, thank you."

She gulped and flicked her eyes in Conall's direction. There was a slight tension in his lips and a narrowing of his eyes, but otherwise his face held the same bored expression from earlier. *Did I answer incorrectly?* Knowing she shouldn't trust the Unseelie king, she wasn't sure how to respond, but at the same time, she was too fearful of what might happen if she turned him down.

"Wonderful. Now, we must discuss this name nonsense," King Corydon replied. *Wow, he doesn't waste any time, does he?*

"Name nonsense?" she repeated.

"Yes. We cannot have an Unseelie princess with a

name like *Lola*." He spat her name as if it were poison rolling around his tongue, his nose wrinkled in disgust. "It isn't proper. It's such a *human* name. When you are at the palace it would only be proper to call you by your given name. Your mother did a wonderful job picking out Ianthe. It honors your Fae background as well as acknowledging your royal eyes." He paused before mumbling, "At least she did one thing right." She studied his expression and could see pain that had turned into rage simmering just underneath his icy exterior.

"But I like my name. Lola is what I've always been called. I was named after my father's mother," she contested without thinking.

His eyes glowed brighter violet and he slammed his fist against the table, causing glasses to fall over and plates to clatter. She jumped, startled. "That human was not your father. I AM YOUR FATHER," Corydon yelled, each word increasing in volume until the last was a deafening roar. She swore she could feel it reverberate through her bones. The servants quickly made themselves scarce, presumably used to that sort of outburst. Conall gripped the table tightly, his knuckles turning white while his eyes widened slightly at Lola, but he still maintained his calm façade.

"I'm—I'm sorry. Of course, you are m-my father." The words were lodged in her throat, but she forced them out in order to placate him. "It's just hard. I've thought of him as my father for the last seventeen years. I can't just change that overnight, but I will try my best to remember. My apologies." *What have I just done?* She was starting to regret the invitation to stay by the minute, and she fought the panic that was quickly rising. Without her elastic to snap, it was more difficult. She counted calmly in her head and tried to breathe in and out, slowly and quietly.

"Of course. Just be sure it doesn't happen again." The

Unseelie king's mood shifted abruptly from his fury back to cold indifference. Conall released his death grip on the table and leaned back in his chair, folding his arms across his chest as he tried to appear unaffected, but she could tell he was upset. *Shit, he's probably pissed at me for upsetting his king.* What little appetite she had reacquired quickly fled her. She didn't even know if she could stomach remaining at the table, but she feared trying to leave would invoke the king's wrath once again.

The men continued their conversation from before as if the outburst had never happened. She caught bits and pieces about their battles with the Seelie, a precarious peace treaty, and infractions against humans committed by their own people. Lola noticed that their conversation dropped in volume when the last topic came up. She would have thought they had forgotten about her entirely except Conall's eyes kept flicking in her direction when the king's attention was elsewhere, like on his plate or his goblet.

She was considering how she could be excused when Conall suddenly stood up. "If you will excuse me, Your Majesty." He bowed as he spoke. "I have matters to attend to about town. I trust my services are no longer required at the moment."

Wait, is he leaving me here with the Unseelie king? Lola shivered at the thought. She didn't want to be left there after the king's violent outburst, and she pleaded with her eyes. She shoved her chair back and stood quickly, feeling her panic and fear rising. The king glanced at her sharply with his nostrils flared and narrowed his eyes slightly. Conall swung his head back in her direction, giving her a slight shake of his head that clearly told her to sit down and pull it together. She tried to subtly take her calming breaths. "Conall…" Her voice shook slightly and the king narrowed his eyes further, a scowl deepening across his face. She cleared her throat. "I believe I left a few things at your home, which I need to gather." She searched his eyes for a sign that he wasn't abandoning her.

"Nonsense." King Corydon waved her off. "I have everything you could possibly need here. Now, if you are leaving"—he turned, addressing Conall—"I must start making arrangements for the court to dine with our princess."

"Your Majesty, I believe it is in your best interest to wait until Ianthe has been exposed to Fae customs before introducing her to the court. I don't believe she is fit to represent you as your daughter or as Unseelie princess just yet. Perhaps if you will allow me to tutor her in our history and her role in the court, I think after a few days I can have her presentable," Conall suggested.

Lola put her hand on her hip and gaped at him. *Not fit to be a princess? Seriously?* She wasn't a savage. She could be prim and proper very easily—in fact, the old Lola had been the epitome of prim and proper, even if a borderline mean girl. She could handle it just fine. She pursed her lips and narrowed her eyes, doing her best to give him the evil eye, telling him he would pay for those comments.

The king turned and looked her over. "Perhaps that is a good idea, but I think Alvina or Rhoslyn would serve her best as a tutor." While the king was looking at her, she glanced over at Conall, who flinched at the mention of Rhoslyn's name. She wondered what that meant. Who was Rhoslyn that she was worthy of such a reaction from Conall?

"With all due respect, sir, while Alvina and Rhoslyn"—Conall spat the latter name as if he was tasting sour milk—"would be wonderful tutors for Fae royalty, I believe they may not have the patience to deal with a half Fae. I think I am the most qualified to teach Ianthe to control her human instincts and emotions."

The king looked her over once more, and she nervously gave him a weak smile. She would much rather have Conall with her as a tutor than Alvina any day, and judging by his reaction to the last suggestion, Rhoslyn would be the last person she would want to meet.

"Very well, Conall. I suppose you may be right about those two. Although they will treat her as the princess she is, I can see where they may not know how to best deal with her." Lola was getting really frustrated with the whole talking about her as if she wasn't there business. "You may start her tutelage this evening. She will not have much time. The town is already buzzing with her arrival, and I'm sure the court is anxious to meet their future queen." Lola blanched at the thought of being the Unseelie queen. "I will give you one week. I'll announce a bacchanalia for her presentation to satisfy the court's curiousity. We all know how much they love a good party. Please notify the staff to make the necessary arrangements."

She searched her brain for the word bacchanalia and seemed to remember them having been particularly interesting when she was studying Greek and Roman mythology. If memory served her well, a bacchanalia was like a drunken orgy. *Oh dear Lord, I hope I'm wrong about that.*

King Corydon turned his attention to her once again. "I trust you can find your way back to your room?"

"Yes, sir," she replied.

"I suggest you don't wander around the castle by yourself. The rooms on your floor are fine, but the main floor is used for conducting business, and it could be very inopportune for you to interrupt royal proceedings. Of course once you have your bearings, you will be required to observe all royal proceedings so you know what is expected of you in the future. The lower level is completely off limits for the time being. Do you understand?" Lola got chills. The Unseelie king was speaking as if she would be living there for the rest of her life, not just a few days like she had in mind.

She wasn't sure what to say to that and certainly didn't want to witness another outburst, so she decided the best way to deal with the situation was to play along for the time being then plan for how she could convince him to let her go back to Aunt Grace. "I understand."

"Good, now that that's settled, I have business to attend to." The king spun on his heels and strode out of the room. She released a sigh of relief that the whole ordeal was over. She didn't want to stay there, not with strangers, especially Unseelie Fae. How she craved to return to her aunt's cottage in the clearing, or even to Conall's warm and welcoming house, not this cold, formal castle.

"Ianthe." Conall's soothing voice pulled her from her thoughts, and she looked up into his sparkling green eyes. His gaze seemed to pull her toward him and without realizing it, she had crossed the dining room and stood next to him. "You must remember everything I told you about the Unseelie. Do you remember?"

"Yes," she whispered.

"I will try to be with you as much as I am allowed, but it will be difficult. You will be on your own at times and you will need to be strong. You cannot show fear in front of them or you will not last a day." His voice was pleading and his eyes seemed conflicted. Leaving her in the lion's den went against all of his protective instincts, but he didn't have a choice. He reached over and traced his finger down her arm, pushing a soothing calm into her.

She sighed. "Thank you. While I don't appreciate you

using your powers on me, I definitely needed that." She felt as if she had just stepped out of the most amazing massage and was completely relaxed. "I will remember to keep my guard up and maintain control of my emotions as best as I can."

"Very well, my flower. I take leave of you now, but I will return in a few hours for your first tutoring session. I suggest you stay close to your room and limit your interactions with the Fae in the castle."

At the thought of him leaving, her panic rose once more, and she fought to push it back down. Conall ran his hands down both of her arms. While the calm washed over her again, she also felt a tingling fire blaze the trail of his touch. Unconsciously, she leaned toward him, her attention drawing away from his hands and back up to his face. His tongue snuck out to wet his lips and she tracked the movement like a lioness tracking her prey. If she just leaned forward a few more inches, their lips would touch. She tipped up onto the balls of her feet, reaching up to close those last few inches. His breathing grew heavy as hers seemed to stop entirely. Abruptly he released her and took a step back. She couldn't help but feel the heavy sting of rejection settling in her heart. *He doesn't want to kiss me.*

"Do you remember how to get back to your room?" he asked her, refocusing her attention on something other than the awkwardness that had suddenly enveloped them. She searched her memory for the route back. He took her hesitation as a no and continued, "Follow me out to the main hall." She followed him from the dining room then followed as he took a left. "Remember, your room is up the grand stairs and to the left, and you are the third doorway to the left. Okay?" He searched her face, not finding the reassurance he was looking for, and frowned. "Ianthe, you must be strong. Remember you are half Unseelie Fae. You are the heir to the Unseelie throne. Everyone else should be beneath you. Act like it."

"Even you?" Lola asked. "Should I act like even you are beneath me, Conall?"

He sighed. "Especially me, Ianthe."

She didn't like the look of resignation on his face. He said her name without any of its usual warmth or cadence. It was flat and emotionless, and she didn't care for it one bit. He turned and started walking quickly toward the door.

"Wait!" Lola called, chasing after him. He turned around and for a brief moment she saw a look of sorrow cross his face before he replaced it with his cool, indifferent mask. He was such a frustrating man. "Can I have my rubber band back before you go?"

"Will you be snapping it against your wrist?" he asked, even though he knew the answer.

She bit her lower lip. He already knew her too well. She needed the comfort and control it offered her, even if he didn't understand it.

His eyes focused on her lips before pulling his own into a narrow line. "No," he stated.

"No?" she repeated, making sure she had heard him right.

"I will not give it back to you if you are only going to hurt yourself again. I told you when we were walking through town what could happen if you did that."

This was not okay. How would she survive without his calming presence and without her coping mechanism? He seemed to notice her inner turmoil, and she heard him sigh.

He reached behind his head and untied the strip of leather that held his hair back. His wavy chocolate locks fell forward, and her breath hitched. If it were even possible, he was more gorgeous with his hair down. She yearned to run her fingers through the strands and see if it felt as silky soft as it looked.

Conall wrapped the piece of leather around her wrist, her skin burning pleasantly where he touched. "There. Use that instead. It won't harm you, but I hope it brings you the comfort you seek." She was touched by his thoughtfulness. She wanted to throw her arms around him and kiss him for all she was worth, but she wasn't going to embarrass herself further. One rejection was enough for her to take the hint that he wasn't interested in her in that way. She glanced down at her wrist, still warm under his leather strap. It was so soft and worn. She rubbed her fingers across it, and when she looked up to thank him, he was gone.

She wondered how long she had stood there looking like a lovesick fool while he left, hoping no one else had noticed their exchange. She turned and walked up to her room with a smile that couldn't be erased.

Chapter 18

LOLA SPENT THE next few hours in her room. She searched the armoire, finding it full of fine gowns in ethereal fabrics. Gorgeous heels lined the bottom as well as another pair of sandals like the ones she was wearing. There were no labels or tags on anything, which made her think everything must have been made by the Fae. Of course, if her father's disgust toward humans was any indicator, he definitely wouldn't want human-made things in his home. The dresser was full of underwear and silky nightgowns, and the makeup brush Alvina had used on her earlier sat on the vanity. She rubbed it against her hand, wondering if the brush itself was magic, but nothing happened. *Must be part of Alvina's magical powers.*

Soon she grew listless and couldn't fight the worry that was gnawing on her bones. How would she escape and find her way home? There was no way she was going to stay there and be an Unseelie princess, eventually becoming the Unseelie queen. The way the Fae looked at her made her as skittish as a rabbit. Maybe she could sneak away in the night. She would have to check to see what guards were there and determine if that was even possible that evening. She glanced at her door and released a sigh of relief when she noticed that the handle locked. At least she could sleep knowing she would be the only one in her room.

She was growing painfully bored when a knock sounded on the door before it was pushed open and Alvina marched across the threshold. "Lady Ianthe, King Corydon would like you to take your meal in your room this evening. I will bring it up when Sir Conall arrives so he can teach you some table manners while he dines with you." Her voice dripped syrupy sweet while delivering the last insult. Lola wanted to sigh; she'd already had a feeling about Alvina, and now she knew she would not find an ally in her.

Before Lola could respond, she heard the click of the door and she was alone again. Her stomach grumbled, and her mouth grew dry. She strolled into the bathroom, thankful to find a glass by the sink, and filled it from the tap. The water was cool and refreshing. As the minutes passed, the boredom increased. Lola grew curious about the castle, but she knew she should not venture out. The more she thought about it, though, the only way to plot her escape would be to get to know her surroundings well.

She crept toward the door, opened it quietly, and peered into the hallway. Thankfully, it was empty. She couldn't remember what was on that floor as everything had seemed to happen in a blur earlier in the afternoon. Since no one was around, she decided to do a little exploring. The king had said that the floor she was on was fine. She looked back at the two rooms before hers then opened the door next to her room. It was another room, and although not as ornate and missing an en suite, it was still plush and gorgeous. She crept closer to the grand staircase, toward the first room—another bedroom just like the previous one. She noticed that the decorations in most of the palace seemed to be of dark colors, while her room was the only thing light and feminine that she had seen.

She approached a door on the opposite side of the hallway, and as she quietly pushed it open, she gasped in surprise. The room was the largest library she had ever seen in a private residence. It was filled with wall-to-wall bookshelves, along with a spiral staircase that led to a second landing full of more books. There were several comfortable-looking oversized chairs in the room as well as an oppressively large table. She walked farther into the library, gawking in awe. There were several magnificent tapestries and paintings hanging around the room. It all reminded her of the Beast's library in *Beauty and the Beast*, and she felt a little like Belle.

A cough startled her from her thoughts. She turned to see an elderly man with shoulder-length white hair and a beard. "Can I help you with something, my lady?" he asked, standing from a chair at a smaller table. He was about the same height as she was, but his frame seemed rather frail, like that of a grandfather. She reminded herself of Conall's advice and turned on the queen bee act she had learned so well in high school. Her mind spun, trying to come up with a response other than, *I was just exploring.*

"Actually, I would be interested in reading about the Unseelie Fae history," she stated coolly, mentally high-fiving herself for her quick thinking. It wouldn't hurt to have some knowledge of the world into which she had been thrust.

The old man beckoned her toward the far end of the room. "Over here you will find the entire section on Unseelie history. Is there anything in particular you were looking for?"

"I'm sorry, but who are you?"

"Oh forgive me, my lady. I am Alfie, the king's scholar. I keep documentation of all the courts proceedings as well as act as historian for His Majesty," he replied with a slight bow. "It's a pleasure to meet you, Lady Ianthe." She scoffed in her head. *Of course he already knows who I am.*

She knew she should probably act like he was beneath her as Conall had suggested, but there was something endearing about the old man. He didn't seem to hold any malice in his expression or show the condescending attitude Alvina had. She went with her gut and answered him politely. "I'm pleased to meet you as well. Honestly, I'm not quite sure exactly what I'm looking for. Mainly I would just like some information to help me, um, adjust."

He smiled kindly at her. "Unseelie history, you said. Well let me see." He traced his fingers along the spines of several books before tipping one back. "This one would be a good start. Of course, I will speak with Sir Conall when he arrives to find out what he will need for your tutoring, but this will definitely get you started." He handed her a large maroon volume. "Please let me know if you have any questions or would like to learn anything else. While Sir Conall is a good fit to teach you about the court, I'm afraid he may be a little rusty on his history. He wasn't a very good pupil." He added the last part with a small frown.

"When you say pupil, do you mean you were his teacher?" Lola asked.

Alfie removed his glasses from his slightly crooked nose and started to polish them against his shirt. If Lola looked closely, she could see evidence that he must have been quite handsome when he was younger. His eyes held warmth, wisdom, and a slight spark of mischief, but what really intrigued her was their enchanting shade of pale periwinkle. "Yes, well, given his unique circumstances, I was given permission to tutor him while he was training for the guard. He was so young and while he was a skilled fighter, he lacked focus in the classroom."

Lola giggled at the thought of young Conall not being able to sit still and pay attention in class.

Alfie smiled at her response. "Hopefully he will be a much better teacher for you than he was a student. If you do find yourself wishing to learn more, you can find me here most days unless I am needed at the court proceedings. I would be happy to teach you."

"Thank you, Alfie. I will see how the tutoring goes and will let you know if I need anything else. I appreciate your help." Alfie looked a little taken aback at her words, and she almost regretted showing her gratitude, but then a huge grin lit his face like a little boy on Christmas morning. *Perhaps I do have an ally in the palace after all*, she thought, leaving the library with the book her hand.

She was so excited after her encounter with Alfie that she forgot to exercise caution in the hallway. She turned toward her room and smacked into a hard body. The impact shook her and she dropped the book with a loud thud. "I'm sorry," she mumbled out of habit.

"There's no need to be sorry," a husky, rich baritone replied. She glanced up to see a fine Fae specimen in front of her. He seemed about her age, but based on what Conall had said, he could have been decades older than her. His straight, jet-black hair was pulled back in a ponytail, accentuating his sharp jaw. She met his eyes with a shock. Two pink irises stared back at her. She had never seen pink eyes before and must have been staring into them for longer than was proper when his low chuckle interrupted her.

"Like what you see?"

She blushed a deep crimson at being caught staring. "I've never seen eyes that color before," she explained, so he wouldn't get the wrong idea.

His pink eyes crinkled with amusement. "Were you just leaving the library?" She nodded. "I hope Alfie didn't bore you to tears in there. I swear that man is getting too old for his job. I'm not sure why His Majesty keeps him around." He added the last part in a haughty whisper.

Lola was about to stand up for Alfie when she remembered Conall's words. "Yes, well, I'm sure His Majesty has his reasons." She rolled her eyes as the old Lola would have when gossiping about someone her friends didn't like.

The boy smiled, and she internally breathed a sigh of relief that she had responded correctly. "I don't believe we've had the pleasure of being introduced. I am Killian." He held his hand out. "A pleasure to meet you, Lady Ianthe."

She hated the way everyone already knew who she was and automatically called her Lady Ianthe. She wished someone would just call her Lola, but she wasn't about to have the king chastise her again. She returned his gesture, placing her hand in his. Instead of shaking it as she had expected, he raised her fingers to his lips and pressed a kiss against her knuckles. While this old-fashioned act from a gorgeous guy would have made some girls swoon, Lola fought the urge to rip her hand away. For some reason, his touch made her skin crawl. She smiled tightly and politely.

"Yes, well, I should get back to my room. I'm sure you have somewhere else to be or something to do," she said, trying to politely excuse herself from his presence.

"I do have some business attend to but would gladly skip it if it meant spending time with you," he replied flirtatiously, tracing his finger down her arm. Little did he know, the act had the opposite effect of what he intended. She fought to not shake off his touch. "I would love to get acquainted with you further," he added in a low whisper.

"I don't think that would be a good idea, Killian," a familiar voice snapped from behind her. Killian dropped his hands and stepped back, narrowing his eyes over her shoulder.

"Don't you need to help your father?" Conall asked. She could feel the anger flowing off of him in waves as he approached.

Killian smiled tightly. "Of course." He turned his attention back to Lola. "I hope we can continue this conversation later." He grinned at her and bent down to retrieve the book she'd dropped. As he handed it to her, their fingers brushed and he paused there longer than necessary. She fought the urge to snatch the book and her hands away forcefully.

"Killian," Conall growled in warning. Killian smiled at Lola once more, dropped his hands then glanced at Conall as his smile turned into a gloating smirk.

"I'll see you around, Lady Ianthe," Killian called over his shoulder, striding confidently toward the grand staircase.

"Ianthe, go to your room—now, please," Conall seethed. She knew the safe thing would have been for her to stay in her room like he said, but she was just so bored. She didn't really regret leaving. Nothing bad had happened; he was just overreacting. The more she thought about things, the more she fumed over his order for her to go to her room. He had no right to order her around. Still, she huffed and headed back, book in hand with Conall trailing behind.

As soon as the door clicked behind them, Lola placed the book on the vanity and rounded on him. "Where do you get off ordering me around?" she hissed.

He was taken slightly aback. "Me? Really? I told you it wasn't safe for you to wander the castle, and what do I find when I return? You swooning in the clutches of Killian. Have you no sense of self-worth?" he spat.

"What is your problem? I cautiously explored the hall-way—so what? I was bored out of my ever-loving mind in here. What did you expect? Me to just sit here and twiddle my thumbs until you returned? I was careful. I only went to the library and then was heading back to my room when I ran into him, and I was definitely not swooning," she retorted. Her cheeks flushed, and Conall couldn't help but notice how beautiful she was when she was angry.

He ran his hands from his face back to his ponytail as he took a deep breath and released it in a sort of half huff, half sigh. "You have no idea, do you? You have no idea of the dangers that surround you. How am I ever going to keep you safe when you make it so damn hard?"

"Who said *you* had to keep me safe? I sure didn't! I didn't ask to come here, and I certainly didn't ask to stay here. I just want to go home!" Her voice cracked as it rose in volume, her despair breaching her anger. She tried to blink back the tears swarming in her eyes but was unsuc-cessful; one escaped and traced its way down her cheek.

He stepped forward and wiped away the tear with his thumb. "I'm sorry, my flower. I know this cannot be easy for you." His sweet words unlocked the storm of emotions inside her and she felt herself cracking. He quickly gath-ered her in his arms, running his hand down the back of her head and through her hair in a comforting gesture. "Shhh, it's okay. I won't let anything happen to you. We will figure this out and find a way to get you home."

A knock at the door startled them both from the intimate moment. Conall instantly stepped back and put some space between them as she spun around, facing away from the door to hide any evidence of her breakdown. Alvina strode in quickly and purposefully, eyes narrowing on the two of them, who probably still stood a little too close for it to be considered proper. Lola wiped her cheeks and eyes, hoping she didn't look like a complete disaster, and schooled her features into haughty indifference.

Alvina cleared her throat. "Lady Ianthe, will Sir Conall be joining you for your meal?" She raised her eyebrow suspiciously at the pair of them.

"How nice of you to think of me, Alvina," Conall replied dryly. "However, I have already eaten. It would be most opportune if you could bring Lady Ianthe's meal so we may begin with her instruction."

"Yes, Alvina," Lola jumped in, remembering the role she now needed to fill. "I would like my dinner as soon as possible, here in my room."

Alvina scanned the two of them again, her tongue prodding the inside of her cheek as she meticulously filed away everything she observed. "Of course, milady. I will bring your meal immediately." She spun on her heels and exited the room, leaving the door open behind her.

"I'm sorry. I didn't mean for that to happen," Lola said quickly, referring to her emotional outburst.

"No need to apologize. In fact, you need to stop that habit. Remember, you are an Unseelie princess—no one but the king should receive your apologies. Everyone else should be the ones apologizing to you, even if you are wrong. In this court, apologizing is seen as a sign of weakness, and you must be conscious of that."

"Of course, I'm—" She caught herself this time before she apologized again "You're right." She sat down on the bed and sighed, thinking of the ever-growing number of the things she would need to remember. Hopefully she had the acting skills to pull this off. She just needed to harness the old Lola—the stuck-up, popular, mean-girl Lola.

He sat down in the chair at the vanity and took advantage of the lapse in conversation to redirect it. "What book did you get from the library? Was anyone in there when you went?" He gestured to the large volume sitting on her vanity.

"Oh yeah, I met Alfie. He seems nice, not your average Unseelie perhaps," she surmised.

"No, you're right about that one. Alfie is not your average Unseelie. In fact, he is not Unseelie at all."

"What do you mean?"

"Well, Alfie is actually a Seelie Fae." Her mouth gaped in surprise. He gave her small sad smile and glanced down at his feet before continuing. "He was a young Seelie scholar who was captured in a surveillance mission. He was tortured for quite some time but had not held an important position in the Seelie court so he had no beneficial knowledge. The Unseelie king did not believe in keeping captives, but his own scholar had recently died and needed replacing. It seemed as a young man, Alfie was interested in all aspects of Fae and had studied both branches diligently, so he had a vast knowledge of our court.

"His early attempts at escape solidified that the only way for him to leave was to die, so he resigned himself to his position. Speaking from personal experience, he is a great teacher." His smile brightened at the last part. "In fact, he is the only person in the palace who I trust. If you should have any issues while I am not here, seek him out, please." He spoke the last few lines looking her straight in the eyes, and she was hypnotized by his forest green gaze.

He broke eye contact and his smile turned down into a frown as he went on, "With that in mind, he should be the only one you trust other than me. Keep your guard up, especially around Killian." His voice turned into a growl at Killian's name.

Lola arched an eyebrow and tried not to let her heart flutter at the thought that he might be a little jealous. "For your information, I did not let my guard down around him." The thought of Killian pressing his lips against her knuckles left cold chills down her spine that she tried to shake off. His frown deepened and his eyes narrowed as he took in her reaction. She shrugged her shoulders. "Something about him makes my skin crawl."

His face looked conflicted, like he was trying so hard not to smile and maintain his serious façade. A sharp knock at the door drew her attention away as Alvina strode in with a covered platter. A thin girl followed behind, carrying goblets and a pitcher. Conall stood as they placed everything on the dresser.

"Here is your dinner. I went ahead and brought an extra glass. If you need anything else, Sir Conall can find me," Alvina stated formally then exited the room with the girl trailing behind.

Conall removed the lid from the platter and examined her food. He picked up the fork and ate a few small bites of things here and there. "Hey!" Lola exclaimed. "That's my dinner. You said you already ate."

"I did. I just wanted to make sure it was prepared as it should be," he stated vaguely.

"Well, can *I* eat *my* dinner now?" she asked, approaching the dresser to grab the platter. Not wanting to get crumbs on the bed, she sat down at the vanity to eat. Conall nodded, handing her the fork, then poured them both a glass of red liquid. She took a bite of her food, savoring the fact that his lips had just touched the fork where her lips were now resting. He sipped his drink while his eyes tracked every movement of her fork and lingered on her mouth. She peered up at him, catching him staring, and he quickly turned the other way, a faint blush coloring his cheeks.

She reached for her glass, smelling the drink to determine if it was wine. It smelled sweet like a floral bouquet with a hint of fruit. She brought the liquid to her lips. It tasted like rosewater, cherries, and sunshine. It was delicious. "Mmm," she moaned. "What is this?"

Conall swallowed hard then replied, "It's ambrosia, a sort of juice or nectar. Drink it slowly—sometimes Fae drinks have a side effect on humans similar to alcohol. While you are only half human, it may still make you a little tipsy." His eyes sparkled with mischievous thoughts. "We can't have you getting drunk while you are supposed to be learning."

He dived into her first lesson, telling her about the different factions of Fae, focusing on Seelie and Unseelie, the two major courts. He explained why they didn't get along, some of the brief history, and gave her information about both of their leaders. She listened attentively while she ate, trying to absorb as much as she could. She hadn't realized how hungry she was until she was scraping an empty plate, although once she thought about it, she really hadn't eaten much that day. Conall smiled, pleased that she had eaten plenty, and placed the empty dishes outside of her door.

She sat comfortably on the bed, listening for the next two hours while he sat or paced around the room while lecturing. Time passed quickly with him as her teacher, although her thoughts weren't always on his lesson, more so on how fit he looked and the angles of his jaw and cheekbones. Before she knew it, she was yawning and fighting to keep her eyes open. She tried so hard not to fall asleep on him or let him think he was boring her, but the events of the previous two days (*has it really only been two days?*) caught up with her.

"Wake up, my beautiful violet flower," his rich baritone whispered in her ear. Lola awoke to see Conall smiling at her and caressing her cheek with the backs of the fingers of one of his hands while the other rested on her shoulder.

She started to apologize for falling asleep on him, but he placed his finger on her lips, silencing her words.

"Remember, no apologies." He winked. "I will leave you to get your rest. You may want to change into something more comfortable before you do. I will be here in the morning and again the evening. I'm afraid I cannot stay with you the whole day. I cannot neglect my other duties and draw unnecessary attention our way." She was disappointed, but she understood. He trailed his hand from her shoulder down to her wrist as he stood, his fingers lingering on his strap, which was tied there.

He frowned, remembering the nightmare she had experienced the night before. "Try to think of me before you sleep, and may it bring you comfort." He pulled his lips into a tight line of worry. "Remember everything I've told you. Good night, my flower. Sweet dreams."

"Thank you, Conall, for everything. I'll see you tomorrow." She yawned.

"Please lock the door behind me."

She nodded, getting up to follow him as he left. When she watched his back heading through the doorway, she noticed his hair was held back not by a leather strap, but by her elastic. A smile lit up her face and she melted a little bit at the thought that he might want to have a piece of her with him. Of course, she quickly scolded herself for being silly and thought he'd simply needed something to hold his hair back since he had given her his leather tie. Her elastic was the logical solution.

She locked the door as he'd requested and listened as his footsteps paused until the lock clicked then picked up again, echoing down the hall. She found a silky nightgown to change into and washed her face before collapsing on the bed. Despite her uneasiness about being left alone in the castle, the locked door brought her comfort, as did Conall's words and strap around her wrist. She traced the soft leather gently, easing her fears and thinking of him until she fell asleep.

CHAPTER 19

LOLA AWOKE TO *find herself back in Conall's cottage. Even more interesting was that she was lying in his bed. She moved to roll over and her hand smacked something hard. Alarmed, she sat up and looked down at where her hand now rested against Conall's chest. She almost let out an embarrassed squeal and quickly peeked under the covers to see she was comfortably covered in her usual tank top and boxer shorts. Looking back at him, she realized he was still fully dressed and resting on top of the covers while she was under them. She smiled realizing it was most likely a conscious decision on his part—he did seem to be quite the gentleman.*

She took the opportunity to memorize the beautiful sight in front of her. She could see his sculpted muscles through his black t-shirt, and he looked peaceful while he was sleeping. His features were breathtaking in the moonlight. His hair—now unbound—spilled across the pillows. She took advantage of the moment to reach over and gently stroke a couple of the silky strands. He sighed and she paused, worried she had woken him. She studied his face, his lips so perfect that she was beyond tempted to press her mouth to his. She wanted to see if they were as soft as they looked. Staring at his mouth, she watched as it quirked up into a smile. Her gaze flicked to his eyes, which were wide open and admiring her in amusement.

"Well this is a pleasant dream," he teased.

"It is, isn't it?" she replied dreamily. She lay back down in the bed next to him, breathing in his woodsy scent, and sighed. "How did I get here?" she wondered aloud, staring at the ceiling of Conall's room.

"You're dreaming. You're not really here," Conall answered.

"Of course I am," she stated disappointedly. Conall's hand grazed hers as he interlaced their fingers. Lola sighed and reveled in the warming calm that was Conall. When he touched her she instantly felt safe, protected, and cherished. It was odd, yet it felt like this was how the world was supposed to be. They both just lay there side by side for hours, fingers entwined, soaking in each other's comforting presence.

A mischievous smile quirked the corner of her mouth.

"What are you smiling about?" he asked with his head turned. How long had he been looking at her like that? She should have felt embarrassed, but instead she felt brave. If this was a dream, she was going to make the absolute best of it.

"I was just thinking," she replied, using his vagueness against him.

"About...?" he prompted.

She released his hand and rolled onto her side so she was facing him and looked into his glittering emerald eyes. "You," she answered on an exhalation, gathering her courage and pushing away her insecurities, her fear of rejection.

He grinned. "Oh? And what about me were you thinking?" he teased, turning his body toward her until he mirrored the way she lay on her side.

"This." Before she lost her courage, she closed the gap between them, pressing her lips against his. They were just as soft and warm as she had imagined. He seemed to take a moment to overcome his initial shock before kissing her back. The change was instantaneous, the kiss ignited as he traced her lips with his tongue. Her breath hitched and he took the opportunity to deepen the kiss. He tasted sweet and a little like pine nuts; it was delicious and intoxicating. One of his hands reached up, tangling in her hair and cupping the back of her neck to pull her closer. His other arm wrapped around her waist, moving his hand against her lower back. She melted against him and bunched her own fists in the front of his shirt, trying to pull him closer.

When she pulled away to gasp for breath, he growled, moving her back into place. He kissed her passionately like he couldn't get enough of her, and she was lost in him. Of all the guys she had kissed before, it had never been like this. She was on fire and would gratefully burn for more. "Ianthe," he said breathlessly, releasing her lips. "My flower." He stroked her cheek, staring at her adoringly. He pressed more soft kisses on her lips and across her cheeks, even one on the tip of her nose. Lastly he kissed her forehead, and then he leaned his head next to hers and breathed in her scent as deeply as he could. She knew exactly how he felt. She wanted to bury herself in his scent and lose herself in his kiss for days.

Snuggled against him in a warm cocoon, her eyes closed contentedly. She felt herself drifting back off to sleep and couldn't fight it no matter how hard she tried. Before she was completely unconscious, she swore she heard him say, "Rest, my love."

She blinked her eyes open, her lips still tingling from his kiss. She stared at the ceiling, wishing with all her might that she were back in Conall's bed and not at the palace. She sighed deeply, relishing the feelings rushing through her body from the most amazing dream she had ever had. She rubbed her fingers back and forth against the soft leather tie on her wrist and closed her eyes, trying to commit every moment of the dream to memory. She was going to try to fall back asleep and continue the dream but then a loud knock sounded on the door.

Alvina pushed it open "Lady Ianthe, King Corydon requests your presence for breakfast this morning in the dining room. It will be served in 30 minutes."

Lola heaved herself out of her reverie and reluctantly went into the bathroom to get ready for the day. Once she had bathed, she looked around to see if Alvina would help her once again, but she was nowhere to be seen. Lola certainly didn't want to be late and risk the king's wrath. She was starting to get a little homesick so she thought perhaps if she wore her clothes, it would help. She found them in the bottom of the armoire, and luckily they had been cleaned. She slipped her jeans and t-shirt on and laced up her boots.

She ran a brush through her hair and stroked the makeup brush from the vanity across her face, hoping some of the Fae magic was still there. She didn't want to get anyone to help her. She smiled, remembering the first pleasant dream she'd had in a while, and skipped down the steps to the dining hall. Upon her entrance, Alvina, who was bringing a tray in, promptly dropped it with a loud clang. The other occupants of the table turned their heads her way with wide eyes.

"Good morning," Lola sang, hoping to lighten the suddenly dark mood that had fallen. King Corydon's eyes narrowed on her. Conall's formal, emotionless mask slipped for a moment and his eyes shone with concern. There were two strangers at the table who stared at her like she was an extraterrestrial. Killian was also there, and he smiled like he was enjoying the awkwardness of the situation.

"Conall, I thought you started her tutoring last night," King Corydon growled, ignoring Lola completely.

Conall turned his attention to his king. "I did, sire. We went over Fae history and heritage."

"Obviously you have yet to get to grooming and dining," the king spat bitterly. A gorgeous blonde narrowed her eyes at Lola, a sadistic smile on her lips. Killian looked as if he were biting his tongue in an effort to refrain from saying something inopportune, and the other man at the table glanced down at his food uncomfortably.

"I apologize, Your Majesty. I was planning to get to those lessons today. Alvina, if you please," Conall said quickly, frowning at Lola. She was puzzled at what she had done to cause everyone to react this way.

Alvina, who had finished picking up what she'd dropped, handed the platter to another servant and quickly walked toward Lola. "Lady Ianthe, follow me," she commanded, leading Lola back toward her room. Once they got up the stairs, Alvina turned on her and glared. "I don't know what you think you're doing, but that was incredibly disrespectful."

"I-I don't understand," Lola stammered.

Alvina rolled her eyes. "You are lucky the king has company this morning, or I have a feeling that conversation would have gone very differently. As it is, you disrespected everyone in that room, and Sir Conall will be punished for your mistake."

"What did I do?" she asked, trying to grasp what had just gone so wrong.

Alvina gestured to her outfit. "You dare to wear human clothes when the finest of Fae garments have been provided for you! You are not fit to be a princess, and I doubt you will become one at this rate." Alvina huffed, throwing open the door to Lola's room and walking straight to the armoire. "While you are staying here, you are to wear only what is provided for you from your armoire and dresser. *These* are the clothes of a princess—what you're wearing is a disgrace. It's worse than the peasants." Alvina grabbed a short pale blue gown with a silver corset. She didn't even wait for Lola to undress before she started tugging Lola's shirt off like she was a petulant child.

"I can do it," Lola hissed, slapping her hands away and removing her jeans. She stepped into the gown as Alvina pulled it up and tightened the corset with more force than necessary. The air whooshed out of her lungs and she was worried she may not be able to breathe in the restrictive garment. Her legs felt a little naked and exposed as the dress hit above the knee, and she looked down at the sweetheart neckline, surprised by the amount of cleavage present. Alvina grabbed her shoulders and made her sit down at the vanity. She picked up the makeup brush and started humming the same tune she had used the day before, this time moving the brush quickly and efficiently over Lola's face and eyelids. Next she ran her fingers through Lola's hair, humming a little louder and twisting a few strands so they fell in beautiful curly waves. "You will need to learn to do this on your own. I am not *your* maidservant," she stated, like the very idea of helping Lola was beneath her.

Lola didn't know how to reply so she just nodded. Finally, Alvina laced up another pair of Greek sandals like those Lola had worn the previous day, except these were silver to match her dress. She gave Lola one more appraising glance and reached toward her wrist to remove the leather strap.

"No!" she exclaimed, slapping her hand protectively over Conall's tie before quickly regaining her composure. "It's fine. I should at least get some say in my accessories." She didn't think she could go back there and face anyone without the comforting leather against her skin.

"Fine, it's your funeral. Let's not keep everyone waiting even longer," Alvina said, tugging Lola by her wrist and practically shoving her down the hall.

CHAPTER 20

LOLA STEPPED BACK into the dining hall, remembering to hold her head high and not show any sign of weakness. The chatter ceased as she approached the table and took an empty seat across from Conall. King Corydon smiled at her, but his smile didn't reach his eyes. It was a pageant smile through and through, only there for show. "I present my daughter, Lady Ianthe," the king said to the Fae gathered at the table.

Lola looked at each of them with a disinterested air. She had met Killian and knew Conall, of course, but had no knowledge of the older man or the beautiful blonde. With her father at the head of the table, Lola sat to his left, Conall to his right. Next to her was Killian and then the older man with hair the same color as Killian's. The gorgeous blonde sat next to Conall, but they both looked as if they would like to be sitting somewhere else. Lola fought pangs of jealousy at the sight of them together. She had no right to be jealous. He wasn't hers, and the night before hadn't really happened; it was just a dream, after all. A slight blush crept across her cheeks at the memory of it, and she dared a glance at Conall, whose eyes swirled from bright green to emerald at the sight of her blush.

"I like your dress, Princess," Killian said, interrupting their moment. "The color is beautiful against your ivory skin." His gaze traveled her body and lingered on her chest in a way that made her wish she were wearing a turtleneck.

Conall frowned. "Lady Ianthe, His Majesty thought it would be best to introduce you to a few members of the court before your bacchanalia. I know you met young Lord Killian last night." Lola looked up at Conall, giving him her full attention after sparing a glance at her father, who appeared intrigued by the fact that she had met Killian already. "This is his father, Lord Dante," he continued, gesturing to the man next to Killian. Lola nodded at him as he did the same to her, and she could see the resemblance to Killian in the shape of his nose and jaw. His hair was the same jet-black shade with slightly more length. The only major difference was his eyes. While Killian's eyes were pink, Dante's were more of a pale orange.

"And finally, we have Lady Rhoslyn." Conall nodded toward the gorgeous blonde with dark green eyes. Lola was sure this woman could be a famous movie star or model. She probably had men falling at her feet. Rhoslyn smiled like a cat who'd caught its prey, and Lola nodded politely once again, trying to ignore Rhoslyn's predatory glare. King Corydon coughed from the head of the table, redirecting everyone's awareness. He sure did like to be the center of attention, but Lola supposed he was used to it with being king and all.

He clapped his hands and announced, "Let's eat." Servants stepped forward from the shadows with overflowing platters of colorful and creative dishes. Lola tried to hide her surprise under a mask of indifference. She needed to act like the old Lola, but it felt wrong. The epiphany struck her to the core: there she was yet again trying to please a father whose expectations she knew she would fail to live up to. It was like déjà vu in so many ways.

Lola was curious as to who Lady Rhoslyn was, but she wasn't about to ask in front of the guests. She would ask Conall later during their lessons. She ate the delicious feast and tried to make polite conversation. As the meal progressed, it seemed Killian had taken quite a liking to her. Several times she caught him staring at her mouth while she ate. Toward the end of the meal, he leaned over toward her and whispered, "I will say. I haven't had a meal this enjoyable in quite some time. It is my pleasure to dine in your presence." He smiled seductively.

She didn't know what was wrong with her. He was beautiful and she was sure his smile could wrap women around his finger and drop many panties, but not hers. For some reason, he gave her the creeps, but she knew better than to let that show. She politely returned his smile. "Thank you." The poor boy took those two words as a sort of encouragement and inched closer to her. Feeling his gaze on her, she quickly lost her appetite and pushed her plate to the side.

Out of the corner of her eye, she saw that he was still fixated on her. She wiped her mouth with a napkin, feeling his stare track the movement across her mouth. When she brought it back down, he reached toward her and rubbed his thumb against her face by the corner of her mouth. "Missed a spot," he explained, though his touch lingered longer than was appropriate. Lola focused on not trying to throw up in her mouth.

Across from them, Conall's brow furrowed and he cleared his throat. "If it pleases the king, Lady Ianthe and I will take our leave to start her morning tutoring."

The king, who had been engaged in conversation with Lord Dante while Lady Rhoslyn flirted with him shamelessly, nodded his head. "Go ahead, Conall. Please see that we do not repeat this morning's incident. It would be most unfortunate. Remember you have other duties to attend to for me as well today."

"Of course, Your Majesty," he replied, standing. She stood as well, hoping to leave, but something caught her hand. She turned back to see that Killian had grabbed it.

"Please let me know if there's anything I can do to help you learn about life in the court, Princess." He stood, bowed slightly, and once again kissed her knuckles. She hoped desperately that he would let go quickly so she could go wash her hands. She smiled politely and once he released his grip, she followed Conall out of the dining hall toward her room.

CHAPTER 21

CONALL CLOSED THE door behind them and took a deep breath. "What were you thinking?" he hissed. "I thought you had learned from the king's outburst yesterday that your human side is not welcome here. Whenever you remind him that you are half human, you remind him of your mother and all she took from him. It stirs his fury. You cannot wear your normal clothes. Don't you get it?"

Lola was taken aback by his anger and frustration. She had only made a simple mistake. "But I hate wearing dresses. You get to wear pants—why can't I? I just wanted to wear something comfortable that reminded me of home." She added the last part in a whisper, finding her voice thick with unshed tears.

His mouth turned down and his anger faded. "I know, my flower, but I'm afraid since you are a princess, you are stuck wearing dresses." She sighed and sat down on the bed. He walked over toward her and ran his hands down her arms, calming and soothing her with his touch. "We must make the best of the situation until we figure out if we can get you home."

It took a minute, but his words sank in. She shrugged off his touch. "*IF*? *IF* we can get me home? No, no, no. There is no *IF*. It should be *when*—*when* we get me home. I am not staying here, Conall, no matter what the king thinks. I have to go back. I need to finish high school and get into college. I have my whole future ahead of me, and it doesn't include becoming the Unseelie queen."

Conall reached toward her once more, this time pulling her into his arms against his warm chest. She took a deep breath, feeling her heart race at his proximity but also feeling as if she had finally come home. His closeness felt just as it had in her dream. "I understand, Ianthe. We will figure it out, but please wait for me to have a plan. I cannot risk you trying this on your own," he pleaded.

"Okay."

He pulled away from her, putting the proper amount of space between them once again. She sighed; of course he wouldn't want to hold her like he had in her dream. "All right, we have much to discuss, and I think it would be best to hold this lesson in the library," he said, opening the door.

The library was bright and quiet, and she didn't even hear Alfie working in there today. She called out his name but received no answer. She looked at Conall, who shrugged. They took seats at the table, and he explained all proper table etiquette (which Lola knew most of from her high society dinners with her dad's clients). Next he explained the king's duties. She had the feeling he glossed over the parts that dealt with humans other than saying he would sometimes have to intervene on behalf of the Fae in dealing with humans and punish those whose crimes against humans became excessive. Lola shuddered, wondering what qualified as excessive to the Unseelie.

"Conall, tell me about the court," she said, trying to direct the conversation away from royal duties of which she hoped to never be a part.

"That's a good one since you got to meet some of them this morning. The court is made of the most powerful Unseelie Fae. These Fae have pure bloodlines, undiluted by humans or other creatures. Take Lord Dante, for instance. His father was the best mind reader in history. He can read human minds and most Fae if he tries." Lola bit her lip in worry. *What if he heard her thoughts about Killian, or her father, or Conall?* Conall noticed the action and guessed the cause of her concern. "He usually doesn't read people because I imagine it would get quite noisy hearing everyone's thoughts all the time." *That's a relief.*

"So, if Lord Dante can read minds, does that mean Killian can too?"

He shook his head. "No, he inherited his ability from his mother." She looked questioningly at him. "I would suggest you stay away from him. It is quite dangerous to be alone with him. He can influence human emotions."

"So he's like you?"

Conall looked outraged at the thought. "No! He is nothing like me. He is a Lampir. He manipulates emotions to paralyze his prey and feeds on human blood."

"Like a vampire?"

"I suppose so. Yes, that's probably the best way to explain it. Do not let him feed on you." His eyes swirled with dark green.

"Gross! Of course not. No wonder he gives me the creeps," Lola said.

"He gives you the creeps?"

"Oh yeah. Whenever he touches me, my skin crawls and I fight the urge to shake his hands off of me." She shuddered. "Even when he smiles at me, it makes me want to throw up. I can tell he's probably used to women falling at his feet, but it has no effect on me."

Conall smiled. "That's the best news I've heard all day. You must be immune to his powers then. I was hoping since you were half Fae he wouldn't be able to influence you like he does humans."

"Okay, that's Lord Dante and Killian—what about the blonde? What was her name?" Lola asked, even though she remembered it, because she wanted to see how he would say it. Would he say it with contempt or sigh it with longing?

"Rhoslyn," Conall huffed. Contempt it was. She smiled in relief.

At that moment, Alfie walked in. "Ah, there you are. Conall, King Corydon said you have urgent matters to attend to."

Conall stood up. "Of course. Alfie, would you please help Lady Ianthe with whatever tutoring she may need? We were just discussing the court."

"I would be honored," Alfie replied. His eyes lit up at the prospect of once again being a teacher.

"Ianthe, I will see you later this evening." Conall bid them both goodbye and left.

"So the courts…" Alfie prompted.

Lola was still trying to get her bearings after Conall's abrupt departure. "Um, yeah, we were just, um, starting to talk about Rhoslyn."

"Ah, that explains it then," Alfie said.

"I'm sorry?" Lola's brow furrowed in confusion.

"Conall's sudden departure. Can you really blame the boy? I wouldn't want to talk about that horrible excuse for a mother," Alfie explained.

"His mother?" she gasped. "The one who abandoned him?" Alfie nodded with a solemn look. *That certainly does explain it.*

Chapter 22

Lola spent most of her day with Alfie, learning everything she could. He taught her about some of the different Fae in the court and who she might expect to see around the palace and meet at her bacchanalia. They ate lunch together and he filled in some holes Conall had left about the history of the Seelie and Unseelie in his lesson the previous night. Lola didn't dare ask him about being a Seelie. She didn't want to bring up bad memories when he was being so kind. She really enjoyed his lesson and felt like she learned a lot, thanking him sincerely when he was called away.

She snuck back to her room and lay down on her bed to read the book she had taken from the library the day before. She felt her eyes drooping and before she knew it, she had fallen asleep.

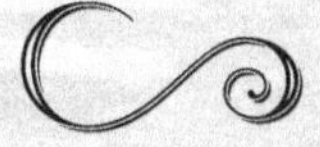

She lifted her head off of the soft mossy ground beneath her. How had she gotten there? She rubbed her eyes and glanced around, trying to orient herself. She was in the middle of the woods, but the last thing she remembered was reading in the Unseelie palace.

She stood up and tried to find a familiar landmark, but nothing looked the same. Suddenly a snapping of twigs to her left sent her heart pounding in her chest. She was debating about running for fear that the boy with icy blue eyes had found her once again when she heard a familiar whisper. "Ianthe." She would recognize that voice anywhere. It didn't matter how many years it had been since she'd last heard it; her heart had memorized it and cherished the memory.

"Momma?" She gasped, turning to her left. Sure enough, there was her mother. She looked as beautiful as the pictures Lola had seen at Aunt Grace's house with her blonde wavy hair and blue eyes. "You can't be here… you…you're…you're dead," Lola stammered.

"I know, sweetheart." Her mother's mouth lifted into a sad, sympathetic smile. "Look at how you've grown. You're such a beautiful young woman. I'm so sorry I wasn't there to help explain things and watch you grow."

Lola's mouth was dry but she managed to nod in acceptance of her mother's words. "I don't have much time, love," Ayanna went on, "and there are some things you need to know." Lola opened her mouth to ask why her mom didn't have much time, but Ayanna continued, not allowing her time to interrupt. "You must always remember who you are. I know it will be tough, but do not let them change you. You are not just Fae, you are human, too. Hang on to your humanity with all you have. Cherish it. Remember, you are the one in control of your destiny, and don't let anyone else tell you otherwise. Your father can be a very persuasive man, so hold true to what you know is in your heart and do not let him bully you into doing anything you don't want to do, including becoming queen." Ayanna placed a warm hand against Lola's cheek, and she leaned into the comforting touch. "There is always another option, but it's up to you to find it. Think creatively and the answer will come to you." Ayanna glanced around nervously. "I'm afraid I must go. Remember everything I have told you, Ianthe. I love you with all of my heart." She rubbed her thumb across Lola's cheek.

"I love you too, Momma. I miss you so much. Please don't go. I need you. I can't do this without you," Lola pleaded.

"I know, honey, and I'm so sorry. You've done so well, and you can do this without me. Besides, you're not alone. You have help. Not all Unseelie are bad. Once upon a time, even your father was an exception, but ruling the Unseelie changed him, and I know my leaving only made things worse. I do not want to see the same thing happen to you." She grabbed Lola in a tight hug. "Trust Conall and Alfie. They will help you. I love you, my Ianthe," she whispered in her daughter's ear.

She released her suddenly and vanished right before her eyes. "Mom?" Lola called. "Momma?!" She looked around to see where her mother could have gone and found it was getting dark. Fear spiked in her mind remembering the night she was attacked in the woods. She started running, not caring where to, just knowing she couldn't stay there.

Finally she saw a break in the woods and stepped into the clearing of her aunt's house. She was so relieved that she was tempted to collapse right there by the edge of the woods, but logic begged her to not let her guard down until she got inside. She jogged toward the house and skipped up the porch steps, pushing the front door open as she called out, "Hello? Is anyone home? Aunt Grace?"

Her great-aunt appeared from the hallway, drying her hands on a dishtowel that she promptly dropped upon seeing Lola. "Lola, is that really you?" Grace put her hand up to her mouth and her eyes began to water.

"Oh, Aunt Grace I've missed you." Lola sighed, falling into her arms. The comforting, familiar touch was all it took to break her down, and she found herself sobbing in her aunt's arms. She told her everything that had happened since the night she'd run away with Conall. Grace listened closely and held Lola tightly, running a soothing hand back and forth across her back. At one point Lola could feel her aunt's tears blending with her own.

"I've been so worried, dear," Grace explained, stepping back from Lola so she could look at her face. "When I woke up and you were gone, I waited, thinking maybe you had gone for an early morning walk. When you still hadn't returned by lunch, I called the police. They said they couldn't do anything until it had been 24 hours and I was about to call your father, but then someone knocked at my door.

"I used to worry about your mother. She would disappear sometimes, and I always knew your father wasn't your biological father, but I never would have thought it would turn out to be the Unseelie king. My goodness!"

"Wait, you said someone knocked at your door," Lola interrupted.

"Oh yes," Grace continued. "One of the Unseelie guards appeared and told me you were safe at your father's palace. Of course, that did little to put my heart at ease, but I was assured you would be treated like the princess you are and I would be able to see you again soon."

"Oh, Aunt Grace, I don't know what to do," Lola exclaimed. She didn't tell Aunt Grace about having just seen her mom in the woods because she still wasn't quite sure what to make of that.

"We'll figure it out, dear. Don't worry." Grace wrapped her arms around Lola once more for a hug.

"Don't cry, my flower." Lola looked around, puzzled to hear Conall's voice in her ear when he was nowhere in sight.

"Lola? Are you okay?" Grace asked.

"I don't know," Lola replied.

"Wake up please, Ianthe." There it was, Conall's voice again. She suddenly felt very tired. She closed her eyes and rubbed them.

When she opened her eyes, she was back in her bed in the palace. She blinked and felt soothing warmth. She tilted her head up and saw Conall's concerned face hovering above her. He reached for her and wiped tears away from her cheeks. Apparently she had been crying in her sleep.

"Why were you crying?" he asked.

"I dreamed I saw my mom again and then I was at Aunt Grace's house." She looked up into his grass green eyes. He didn't seem surprised—which was an interesting reaction—so she continued, "It just felt so real. I swear, Conall, it was like they were both here hugging me."

His lips drew into a tight line. "I suppose it's time we talk about your Fae heritage," he stated.

"But we've already studied Fae history," she countered as she sat up.

"No, not Fae history, your Fae *heritage*. Ianthe, it's time I told you about your magic."

Chapter 23

"M Y MAGIC?" LOLA parroted.

Conall sighed and nodded. "I was hoping to postpone this conversation to another time, but after what you just told me, we need to have it sooner rather than later." She swung her legs over the side of the bed so she was sitting next to him. She had a feeling she would need to borrow some of his soothing comfort soon. "Ianthe, how many of these vivid dreams have you had?" he asked.

"Um…quite a few, I suppose."

"Did they start after your seventeenth birthday?"

She thought for a moment and then grimaced, realizing the vivid dreams had started when her nightmare started. She nodded her head yes, unable to find the words to tell him about that specific dream.

"Can you tell me about them? The other ones, not the one you just had?"

She swallowed and nodded her head again. It took her

a few minutes to gather her thoughts and courage. "Well, most of them have been nightmares about this party I went to."

"Nightmares?" His lips pressed together into a white line. "Does this party have anything to do with why you snap that band around your wrist?" He traced his finger around the leather strap that now encircled her wrist.

"Yes." She paused. "I was…um…attacked at the party." She felt the absence of his finger on her skin as he clenched his fists against the bedspread. She didn't want to upset him further by going into the dirty details. "It's okay, someone heard me call for help, so he didn't hurt me that badly. I only had a few bruises." She swore she heard Conall release a faint growl at that last bit.

"Since it happened," she went on, trying to ease his worry, "I have nightmares of that night and they feel as real as when it happened. I also had one after I was attacked in the woods, and then I've had some very realistic dreams with—" She blushed and paused. How could she tell him about her dreams about him? How would he react?

"With what, Ianthe? I can take it. Tell me," he demanded.

"Um…with…you," she whispered, staring at her hands as her face heated.

She risked a glance at his face, and his demeanor had instantly changed at her words, his scowl turning into a bright smile. "Of course. It all makes sense now."

She quirked an eyebrow. "Oh it does, does it, Spock? Care to share with the rest of the class?"

"Well, I believe your magic powers lie in your dreams. You're a Mara."

"A Mara?"

"Yes. Maras have the power to control the dreams of others. Unseelie Maras tend to cause people to have night terrors and feed off of the fear." Lola winced. She didn't like the sound of that. "Seelie Maras, on the other hand, usually use their abilities to inspire people like muses that artists claim come to them in a dream." *Well, that is definitely a better way of looking at things.* "Your powers aren't quite the same as the average Mara. For some reason, perhaps due to your mother's side, you don't merely enter people's dreams, but rather you call them into yours," Conall explained.

"I *call* them into my dreams?" she inquired.

"Yes. The dreams you had about me were dreams we shared. Most of the time I would find myself suddenly pulled into your dream without realizing it. It felt real to me as well." He gazed into her eyes, attempting to quiet any of her fear or embarrassment.

"Then my mom—"

Conall rubbed his chin. "It could have been just a normal dream or something else. The world is full of mysteries that even we cannot explain." "So if I call people into my dreams, does that mean I'm responsible for my nightmares? That I've been pulling that...*him* into my dreams just to torture me?" Her panic began to rise.

Conall wrapped his hand around her upper arm, pushing a calming surge through her. "It's not like you meant to do it, Ianthe. You just need to learn how to control it. It usually helps if you focus on something calming before you sleep"—a grin crept across his face—"like how you thought about me before you fell asleep last night."

She blushed an ungodly shade of red and stared at her lap. He sensed her embarrassment and placed his other hand under her chin, tipping her head back up to make direct eye contact with him. "I did not say that to embarrass you, my flower. I said it because it was the best dream I have ever had." His intense gaze flicked down toward her mouth as she chewed on her lower lip. Was she imagining things or did he look like he wanted to kiss her? Maybe pick up where they'd left off in her dream? He leaned forward, lost in the moment, and she met him halfway, pressing her lips against his and breathing in everything that was Conall. The kiss was even more incredible in person than it had been in her dream. She lost herself in him and yanked on his shirt to pull him closer. Once his chest pressed against hers, she wrapped her arms around him, reveling in the feel of his muscles rippling underneath her hands and the sweet earthy taste of his lips.

A sharp knock on the door thrust them back into reality and she felt Conall jump from the bed and stride toward the bathroom. Alvina appeared with Lola's dinner. "I thought Sir Conall was with you." Lola prayed Alvina couldn't see the blush spreading across her face or the way her fingers twitched, itching to press against her lips, which still tingled from the pressure of his kiss.

She heard the faucet run in the bathroom and Conall returned with a glass of water that he sipped casually, leaning against the doorway. "I am, Alvina," he stated, maintaining his indifferent demeanor.

"Of course," Alvina grumbled. "I brought an extra plate as King Corydon said you require to be fed." She placed the plates on the vanity and left only to return a moment later with a pitcher and goblets. "If you need anything…" She trailed off, not really intending for them to bother her as she left the room for the evening.

Conall walked over to the vanity, grabbed his plate, and sat across the room from Lola. A pang of disappointment struck her chest, but she schooled her features, refusing to let him see it. They both ate in silence, seeming to stew in their own thoughts.

Finally, he interrupted the quiet. "Ianthe, I'm sorry I kissed you." *What the hell?* Of all the things he could have said, she certainly wasn't expecting that. She closed her eyes and chewed on her bottom lip, either trying to control the pain his words caused or trying to stop herself from lashing out in anger—she wasn't sure which. "It wasn't my place to do that, and it cannot happen again. You are a princess, and even as the king's first in command, I am still his servant. It is not proper and could be punishable if it were to be discovered." The pain just kept coming, and she didn't know what to say. She was afraid if she spoke her voice would betray the emotions she was trying to hold at bay. She rubbed the leather strap around her wrist and pulled it back, but it didn't snap like her elastic. There was no physical pain to replace the emotional pain, and she sighed in frustration.

"I understand," she started, but her disappointment and acceptance bled into anger. She'd had her fill of accepting the events life or fate or whatever you want to call it threw at her without complaint. "Actually, you know what? I don't understand. If I'm the 'princess', shouldn't I have a say in who I choose to kiss?" She used air quotes around the word princess because she certainly didn't feel like one, and the Fae's antiquated views of the world were starting to piss her off. This wasn't *The Princess Diaries* where she would find a loving grandmother she hadn't known she had and enjoy learning all that came with her newfound royalty. She wanted no part of ruling these malicious creatures, especially not after what she had read about them. Her stomach rolled when the thought struck like a knife to her gut. She was one of those malicious creatures—at least half of her was. She swallowed past the thickness in her throat and shoved that thought as far down as it could go. She couldn't even begin to start processing that right then—not with Conall sitting in front of her explaining things she should probably be listening to, things she may need to know in order to survive.

"It doesn't work that way here. You will understand soon," he replied with the most pathetic attempt at a smile she had ever seen.

"Oh, that answer wasn't vague in the least bit," Lola bit back, her voice seeping with sarcasm to disguise her inner turmoil. "Fine, Spock. You want to play games, we'll play games."

Conall huffed. "I'm not playing games, my flower. These are the rules we both must follow."

"Rules are always part of the game, Conall," she replied bitterly, narrowing her eyes. "And as long as we are following the rules, don't you think it's unwise to call me your flower?" She regretted the words as soon as they left her lips. She adored his nickname for her and loved hearing it roll off his tongue, but it was too late to take it back. If he wanted to pretend like the attraction or feelings or whatever it was between them didn't exist, she could play too.

He flinched when he heard the words, and she almost opened her mouth to apologize but then he abruptly stood. "Your bacchanalia is quickly approaching, Lola." She fought a small smile at the fact that she'd made him agitated enough to revert to using her human name. It reminded her of their little spat before they ever came to the palace, before things had changed so drastically. She found herself wistfully longing to go back and not let the king discover her in Conall's cabin that morning.

"We have much to prepare for. We will look at your

dining etiquette tonight, and any tutoring along the lines of your queenly duties will be taken over by Alfie from now on. Let's move to the dining hall for this lesson." He opened the door and exited quickly, expecting her to follow. Of course, she complied. She barely contained the urge to stomp in retaliation on the way down there, but she could play his game well. He probably didn't know she had been playing these sorts of games for a long time, so she plastered on her best pageant smile and pretended like she didn't have a care in the world.

Once they reached the dining hall, which thankfully was empty, he motioned toward a chair with a place setting ready and instructed her on all the different utensils and their uses, as well as proper table manners. She rolled her eyes at him during the last part of the lesson. She had very good table manners, thank you very much. She hadn't realized she had tuned him out until he snapped his fingers impatiently.

"Lady Ianthe, did you hear me?"

"Yes of course, Conall," she replied, plastering the sickly sweet smile back on her face.

Apparently that was not the answer or reaction he was hoping for. "In that case, I will see you in three days. Alfie will take over your tutoring in the meantime and when I return, we will make sure you are ready for your bacchanalia."

Wait, what? He's leaving me here—alone?

Her fake smile faltered as she tried to contain the panic. She didn't want him to see it, didn't want him to know how much she really needed him when he clearly didn't feel the same. He gave her a short, formal bow and left her sitting in confusion. Clearly playing games had not garnered the response she was hoping for. She walked up to her room and got ready for bed, trying to figure out where things had gone wrong. When she lay down to go to sleep, she tried to clear her mind, but the last thing she remembered was wishing that this time, she wouldn't see Conall in her dreams.

CHAPTER 24

LOUD BASS MUSIC *thumped through the air and vibrated her bones.*

Shit—the party house.

While she didn't really want to see Conall, she certainly hadn't meant to come back to this place. She tried to remember what he's said about being a Mara. She would have to ask Alfie about it the next day and see if there was a way to control these dreams of hers.

There was a slight difference in the scene that night. Instead of feeling pulled to repeat the same events, she felt more like an outside observer, free to move where she pleased within the dream. With this in mind, she made a conscious effort to turn toward the street instead of walking to the house. She walked past the cars lining the driveway and down the block, not noticing the fog creeping in around her until it was affecting her vision. No longer able to see clearly in the distance, she turned to glance back at the house, but that too had faded in the fog.

"Pull it together. No freaking out, Lola. This is your

dream. You can control it," she reassured herself as her *trepidation spiked. She continued walking, trying to regain control when she heard his voice. "Little one…come out, come out, wherever you are,"* he called, mimicking the me-*lodic tune she had used as a child when playing hide and seek.*

No, no, no.

She didn't want him here. How had he gotten there? How was she pulling him in, and more importantly, how could she stop? She turned in a circle, trying to figure out the direction from which the voice originated.

"Did you think you could just forget about me, or that I would forget about you?" He clucked his tongue. *Tired of just standing there, she picked a direction and started running. "Tsk, tsk, little one. You cannot escape me." His voice seemed closer. "I am everywhere," he whispered in her ear.*

She gasped in surprise and reached her hand down, hoping to snap her elastic and wake herself up, only to find Conall's leather strap instead. She dug her nails into her wrist next to the strap and felt the biting sting but still couldn't get herself to wake up.

"Who are you?" she yelled, *tired of being the fright-ened little mouse in this scenario. She spun around and met his icy blue stare head on.*

A slow smile spread across his lips and his sharp teeth glinted in the moonlight. "Wouldn't you like to know," he teased. "Shall I tell you?" He trailed a finger down her arm, causing bile to rise in her throat. She fought to not shudder and give him the satisfaction of knowing how much his touch repulsed her. "No, I think this is much more fun. Besides, you will find out soon enough."

She knew he was Fae, and perhaps he was Unseelie?

From the way he enjoyed torturing her and tasting her fear, she was almost sure that he was. She narrowed her eyes at him, showing her displeasure.

He chuckled, amused. "Ahh, always such a treat, little one. Shall we have another taste? I've been craving you since our last encounter."

"Don't touch me," she hissed, suppressing her gag reflex. "Leave me alone!" As soon as the words had left her mouth, he vanished with a look of shock upon his face.

• • •

Lola woke with a start, sitting straight up in her bed. She clutched her hand to her chest, trying to calm her racing heart. Despite the fear that still coursed through her veins, she was relieved. In the end, she had made him disappear. She didn't know how, but she was sure the only reason he'd vanished was because she had wanted it, possibly because she had even said it. Maybe there was a way to control her powers and not let them control her. After she cleared her head, she lay back down and willed herself to sleep. This time, she did not dream.

CHAPTER 25

THE NEXT MORNING when she went down for breakfast, she was surprised to see that Corydon was the only one at the table. They ate in uncomfortable silence; he was studying some sort of document, and she was too nervous about saying the wrong thing or doing something to elicit his ire. When she had finished her meal and asked to be excused, he didn't even deign to give a verbal response, only a simple nod.

The palace—or castle, as she liked to call it—felt emptier without Conall there. Alfie spent a large chunk of her day going over her duties as a princess and future queen (which she had no desire to become). He was kind and pleasant, but his lessons were a little dry and she had the bad habit of daydreaming like she did when the teachers at school droned on about something she didn't see the importance of. Why would she need to know what she would have to do as queen if she never intended to become one?

She had lunch with Alfie and dinner was served in her room. Apparently, even though he'd said nothing to her at breakfast, her father thought her etiquette could still use some work. Unfortunately that meant someone needed to go over it with her, and Alvina was given the task. Neither of them was too pleased about that.

Alvina had little patience for her and treated her as if she was an imbecile, incapable of ever filling the new role that had been thrust upon her. Thankfully, she only needed her assistance that one night. The next day, over another silent breakfast, her father apparently found her dining skills to be adequate.

In those few days without Conall, a few things became blaringly evident. First, it didn't matter that she was Corydon's daughter; the fact that she was half human never went unnoticed. She could see it in the disgust etched on Alvina's face any time she had to do something for her, in the way a few of the guards watched her with hungry eyes, and in the way Lady Rholyn stared daggers at her over dinner.

Second, Killian was an insatiable flirt who had his eyes set on her, and he didn't seem to have the same qualms about her position as Conall did. He never was overly flirtatious with her, more like being a shameless flirt was part of his personality. He made it his goal to see how many times he could make her blush or fluster her over dinner, and she made it her goal to reveal nothing. She wished she could say she was the winner of that game, but that would be a lie. Thankfully while King Corydon would tolerate Killian's actions over dinner, he was quick to shut down Killian when he offered to walk Lola back to her room, which she was thankful for. The next book she would ask Alfie for was one on Lampirs.

Her lessons were going well. She even managed to get a quick breakdown on the hierarchy to understand why Alvina called Conall "Sir Conall" even though Conall classified himself as a servant to the king. His position as first in command was a high honor that some coveted and while it did not place him at the same rank as a lord like Killian or his father, Dante, it did place him above the regular servants like Alvina. All the politics of it reminded her of a couple period shows she had seen on PBS and Comedy Central. Apparently Alvina was like the head housekeeper of the castle, the one who ordered around all of the maids and personally tended to the king's demands. It made sense with her bossy and holier-than-thou attitude.

The more the days dragged on, the more she missed Conall, his smile, and his comforting touch. She missed his gorgeous soft locks and glittering emerald eyes. In the time he was gone, she realized how comforting his presence was, how much she valued the knowledge that someone would have her back. Many times she felt like a small fish swimming in shark-infested waters.

She tried not to think of him at night before falling asleep so she wouldn't call him into her dreams. She had also worked with Alfie on focusing her Mara ability in their time together, which helped break up the monotony of the dry lessons on the politics and expectations. He had her practice meditation as well as imagining taking control of any situation. The lessons seemed to be helping because her last night before Conall's return was spent in Aunt Grace's cottage enjoying the company of her aunt without actually being there. She told Grace everything (minus the make-out sessions with Conall and the confusing emotions she felt for him), and Grace was relieved to be able to check in on her at night through their shared dreams. In a world where everything else seemed to be spinning around her, it was nice to finally feel in control, especially when that control kept the nightmares at bay.

CHAPTER 26

FINALLY, THE DAY of Conall's return was upon her. As much as she tried to deny it, her heart fluttered at the thought of seeing him again. Had he missed her as much as she'd missed him? Had he thought of her at all? Her excitement dimmed the minute she stepped into the dining hall for breakfast with Corydon to discover a table full of people. Among the small crowd, she recognized Killian, Lord Dante, Lady Rhoslyn, and lastly, Conall. A smile lit her face when her eyes landed on him and she fought the urge to run and throw herself into his arms. Remembering that she was in front of the king and the court, she schooled her features and reminded herself that she should still be mad at him for leaving her without an explanation. Okay, maybe the explanation bit was her fault for not paying attention, but still. His eyes twinkled at her initial reaction, but a frown tugged his lips down as her smile faded.

King Corydon introduced her to the rest of the court before beginning their meal then she took a seat next to him at the head of the table. Killian was on her other side with Conall across the way. Throughout the meal, Killian spoke excitedly about her upcoming bacchanalia. He flirted with her, finding ways to touch her casually by bumping against her. She was nothing but polite, with her pageant smile on full beam.

Her father looked pleased. "We have decided that tomorrow night would be the perfect evening for your bacchanalia. After speaking with Alfie last night, I think you're ready," he announced. Lola tried not to choke on the juice she was drinking.

"Are you sure, Your Majesty? There are many things we still need to cover, including dancing, and with my additional duties, I may not have time today," Conall interjected.

"Yes, I'm sure. I'm confident you will find some way to make the time for it," the king replied coolly.

"I could teach her," Killian volunteered while the murmur of the rest of the crowd rose excitedly.

"Very well, Killian. I trust you to teach her all the proper steps. Keep in mind that she is your princess," King Corydon stated.

"Of course, sire," Killian replied.

Lola huffed, annoyed by the fact that no one bothered to ask her for her opinion on the matter. She didn't care for anyone making decisions that should be hers, and she certainly had no desire to dance with Killian. The thought of him holding her made her uneasy. If she had to dance with anyone, she would much rather it be Conall, even if she was still mad at him. She glanced up from the table at him, and he was staring daggers at her side. If looks could kill, Killian would already be dead. Her heart panged with the hope that perhaps his expression was due to jealousy.

They all finished the meal with polite conversation then King Corydon took the rest of the Fae to another room to conduct business. Conall approached her before he was called to join them. "Don't let him try anything," he growled, voice low. Shooting one last look of contempt in Killian's direction, he hesitantly followed the rest of the court from the room.

"Come, Princess, your ballroom awaits." Killian smiled slowly, offering Lola his elbow as he led her from the room. They went to a part of the palace she had yet to see since she mainly stayed on the upper floor for her own safety. She gasped when they stepped into a large, ornate ballroom decorated in rich reds and golds. Killian went over to what looked like an old phonograph player and turned a crank until music began to play. "Of course, for your bacchanalia, there will be a live band, but we must make do with this for now." The castle always felt old, like she had stepped back in time, but a phonograph! She stifled a giggle as he extended his hand.

She placed her hand gently in his, hating the goose bumps that dotted her flesh. He led her through the steps of a waltz, all the while maintaining polite conversation and even laughing with her when she accidently trampled his toes. He seemed nice enough; perhaps Conall was wrong about him. Sure, at times he still gave her the creeps with his touch, but he was friendly enough and nothing but kind to her. She was debating his merits when suddenly the music changed and he pulled her close to his chest.

She wasn't expecting the motion and stumbled against him. Regrettably, he took that as encouragement to pull her even closer. Her heart thudded, but not like when she was held close by Conall. Something didn't feel right about this. She took a calming breath and inhaled Killian's scent—sweet and smoky. "This feels right, doesn't it?" he crooned in her ear. "I could make you very happy, Lady Ianthe. I know the Unseelie well. I know the court well. It would be a beneficial match."

Lola was still processing his words when she felt him nuzzle her neck. How had she allowed things to spiral out of control so quickly?

He inhaled her skin and moaned, "You smell utterly divine." Her eyes shot wide and her heart picked up speed. The involuntary quickening of her heart rate drew his attention to the pulse point on her neck. He pressed a kiss right on top of it, and she was very quickly remembering just what kind of Fae he was.

"Killian, what are you doing?" she asked nervously. She felt his tongue trace along her skin and she struggled to escape from his hold, but he only gripped her tighter.

"Just one little taste, please, Ianthe. I can't stand being this close to you and not tasting you." His teeth scraped across her skin and she fought harder.

"No!" She shoved against him with all her might and he growled in response. "Let me go!"

Killian released her so suddenly that she fell on her butt with a painful thud. Dazed, she looked up to see Conall holding Killian off the ground by his throat. "She said no," he seethed. Killian struggled to breathe. *This isn't good.* As much as Killian deserved it, she now understood the workings of the Fae court and knew Conall's rank was below Killian's, meaning he could be punished for attacking someone above his stature without an order.

"Conall, it's okay. I'm fine. Let him go, please," she pleaded. Realizing what he was doing, he abruptly released Killian, who gasped for breath with a murderous expression on his face.

"Killian, thank you for teaching me how to dance. I appreciate it and would be honored if you would save me a dance at my bacchanalia," Lola stated sweetly with her best pageant smile in place.

Both guys appeared confused at her interjection and the sudden change in topic, but it worked. She had sufficiently diffused the situation. Killian stood up and brushed himself off. He smiled seductively at her, which had the opposite of its intended effect and made her feel dirty. "Of course, milady, it would be my pleasure." He approached Lola and kissed her hand. Despite the tremors that threatened to rack her body, she smiled politely and held her head up high as he turned and exited the ballroom.

Once he left, she risked a glance at Conall. He stared at her like she was a three-headed alien. "He almost bites you and you ask him to dance with you?!" he roared.

"I had to do something. You were about to kill him, and if you had really hurt him, he could have reported it to the king," she explained. The last of her calm had vanished and the tremors that had threatened to take over before conquered her. Her hands shook and her knees almost gave out. She raised a hand to her neck where Killian's teeth had scraped her skin.

Conall's whole demeanor changed in an instant. His anger was forgotten and his only concern was for her. He rushed to her side and pulled her into a comforting embrace. With her against his chest, the soothing calm seeped off of his body directly into hers in waves. He took a deep breath, and she breathed with him. He repeated this several times until Lola stopped shaking. "I'm sorry, my flower. I was so worried he had hurt you," he whispered into her hair. She sighed at the term of endearment and soaked in every second of the embrace that he would allow. She felt his lips press against the top of her head and extra warmth surged throughout her body. His arms had become her safe place.

After some time, they both stepped apart, remembering where they were—in the open ballroom and easily in view of anyone walking by. "Thank you, Conall." She swallowed hard, shoving down the mixture of conflicting emotions. "I think I want to lie down for a bit."

"Very well, I'll check on you later," he replied, and she left the ballroom, heading to her room on shaky legs. Once there, she collapsed onto her bed and broke. She sobbed into her pillow for everything that was threatening to overwhelm her—for being related to a cruel Unseelie king, for being taken away from the one family member who seemed to really care about her, for being attacked in the woods, for being wanted and rejected by Conall, for feeling unwelcomed by Alvina and Rhoslyn, for almost being bitten by Killian, whom she had been starting to trust—for everything. She cried herself to sleep and dreamed of drowning in her tears.

CHAPTER 27

LOLA SPENT THE rest of the day in her room, telling Alfie she didn't feel well when he came to ask about their lesson. His kind eyes spoke of understanding. "I know this must be hard for you, Lady Ianthe. If there is anything I can do to help, please don't hesitate to ask," he offered, turning to leave.

"Wait," Lola called. She had been thinking more and more about this, but wasn't sure how to approach the subject. She twisted her hands in her lap nervously and played with Conall's leather tie on her wrist. "Um, Alfie, is there any way I can get out of this?" Poor Alfie looked so confused, and she knew she was going to have to spell it out for him. "I don't think I can be the Unseelie princess, let alone their queen. I want to go back to my life—my human life."

She was tired of fathers making decisions for her, tired of living in that castle, tired of the tiptoeing around on eggshells, tired of trying to be someone she was not, and more than anything, she was tired of being the pathetic, scared little girl who always seemed to be in tears. She realized in order for anything to change, for her situation to improve, she needed to change. She needed to find the strength and wit to rescue herself. While others may be able to help, she wouldn't depend on anyone else to save her. It was time she took what she'd learned in her dreams and applied it to real life. It was time she took control.

Alfie sighed and pulled out the chair by the vanity. "I was afraid this would be too much for you, but I must say, I'm also relieved." She looked up from her wrist at the last part.

"Relieved?"

"Yes, my dear." He smiled sadly. "You are far too good for this life. The things you will see…they will change you. I fear for what the Unseelie will make of you, what you will become if you stay. You will no longer be the caring young woman sitting in front me, and that would be a great tragedy." Alfie sighed again. "I have been performing a bit of side research," he admitted, smirking at her mischievously before continuing. "You do have a choice, my dear. While most Unseelie would murder to be in power—and many have—you do have a choice. If you choose to formally abdicate the throne with just reasons, the court may rule to accept it. Of course, your father will not hear of this. If he even hears whispers of the word abdicate, he will lock us both up until he breaks you and remolds you into the queen the Unseelie need. I fear that may be worse than death for you."

She gulped. She had seen Corydon's rage and, no doubt, his only daughter turning down her spot as his heir would cause him to lash out immensely in a way she couldn't quite predict.

"All great choices are made with great risks. You must

decide for yourself if the consequences are worth the actions you are willing to take. If you do decide to abdicate, I would strongly suggest you do it publically so the king cannot manipulate the court into believing otherwise. I cannot say exactly what will happen to you after that. There are too many possibilities and it is probably naïve to think the Fae and your father will leave you alone for the rest of your life. I'm sure there will be certain fallout we cannot predict, but you are powerful, Ianthe, more powerful than you realize. You can do this, if it is what you want. We will need to do some extensive planning, but if this is what you want, I will help."

Finally, someone was offering to help. Someone was offering her a way out, which she so desperately longed for. "Yes, Alfie, that is what I want."

"Of course, milady. I will start gathering what you will need. It will probably take a few days, and don't tell *anyone* of our plans just yet."

"Not even Conall?" She was slightly bewildered. She would trust Conall with her heart and her life, so why not with her idea to escape?

Alfie frowned. "I'm afraid not, Lady Ianthe. I'm not sure how he will take the news of your plans to leave." He released his breath in a huff, assessing her reaction to his words. "Don't fret, dear. We will tell him when the time is right, but I don't want him to know until we have everything in place. I worry King Corydon may sense his shift in loyalties, and it could be the end of us all."

The truth of Alfie's words resonated within her. "You're right. I will do my best to hide it from him," she replied, attempting to reassure him.

"You must keep it from him. It could mean death for all of us, or worse." His face was so grim that it gave Lola pause in her plans. What if it didn't work? She didn't think she could live with herself if she was the reason something happened to Alfie. She had grown to care for him; he had become her Dumbledore. She didn't even want to consider the possibility of something happening to Conall because of her. That would shatter her.

"One more thing, Princess." His words tugged her from her dark thoughts. "If you have any acting skills at all, you will need to utilize them. Has Conall told you anything about your bacchanalia?"

"He said there will be a grand feast and dancing."

He shook his head dejectedly. "I didn't suppose he would want you to know. I, however, feel it is imperative that you prepare yourself, so you won't be caught off guard." Her brow furrowed in puzzlement. "You see, the bacchanalia is traditionally a festive celebration with both humans and Fae."

"Humans?" she asked excitedly, but Alfie's expression stopped her cold.

His lips drew into a tight line. "Yes, humans will be there…as entertainment." He seemed to be dancing around the facts as not to disturb her.

"Like playing music?" she asked, hoping that was the kind of entertainment he meant. She knew from some of the folktales she had read how much the Fae loved to listen to humans create music.

"Yes, the musicians will be human, but there will be other humans as well. The Unseelie Fae feed off of humans, whether it be their talent, their emotions, or otherwise…" Alfie trailed off, but Lola understood as her memory of Killian's teeth scraping her skin flashed in her mind, and she shuddered. "You have to understand that it is how they function, how they survive. Sure, there are ways to feed on humans without causing them damage or pain, but most Unseelie view humans as toys or food, similarly to how humans view cattle, and then there are also Fae who enjoy tormenting and feeding off darker emotions like pain and despair.

"Of course, Seelie Fae are not without their faults. At a bacchanalia, some cause humans to sing until they lose their voices, play instruments until their fingers bleed, or even dance until they drop dead from exhaustion. Fae food and drink also affect humans differently, causing immediate addiction in some cases or alcohol poisoning in others if they have too much. The Unseelie, however, and especially some of the court, have darker desires where humans are concerned. You will see things that may disturb you, but you cannot let it show. You cannot let anyone sense your disapproval, disgust, or fear. Do you understand?"

Lola nodded her head and swallowed hard. She remembered how some of the Unseelie had hungrily watched her that first day in the village when her panic and fear had spiked, how the one with icy blue eyes had commented that her fear was delicious and called her his prey. She understood Alfie all right, but it would take everything she had to act like the haughty princess King Corydon wanted her to be when all her instincts would be screaming otherwise. She knew it would be imperative to her own survival. She must do everything in her power to remain calm and appear indifferent. "I understand, Alfie. Thank you for the warning."

"All right." Alfie patted her on the knee in a grandfatherly gesture and rose to leave. "I bid you good night. I will start on our plan and in the meantime, to keep suspicion away, you should act like the Unseelie princess His Majesty wants you to be. If you need anything, you know where to find me." He walked toward the door.

"Alfie," she called, and he turned back to her. "Thank you. I know you're risking a great deal to help me, and I haven't done anything to deserve it." She saw he was about to argue with her, so she quickly finished, "But I appreciate it. You are truly one of a kind." He bowed and smiled at her before leaving her room.

Conall did not return to her room that night. She had thought perhaps he might, since it was the night before her bacchanalia. She wondered how he expected her to act the next night if she wasn't warned ahead of time about what she may encounter. Perhaps he thought he was protecting her by not saying anything, but she was glad that Alfie had explained. She wasn't sure how she would take seeing Unseelie manipulating and possibly even torturing humans, but now she could at least prepare herself for the worst. She practiced her meditation while imagining the worst possible scenarios she could encounter, but never could she have possibly imagined what would actually unfold.

CHAPTER 28

THE NEXT MORNING Lola woke up refreshed. The previous night she had focused all of her energy on Aunt Grace before she fell asleep and spent her dreams at Grace's house, telling her about their plan to abdicate and escape. Naturally, Grace was worried about the consequences, but Lola could see the relief in her eyes. She didn't want her to become the Unseelie queen either.

The palace was a bustle of excitement as servants dashed back and forth decorating, setting up furniture, and cooking in anticipation of the bacchanalia. She grabbed breakfast from the kitchen and dined alone in the dining room, her father overseeing the preparations for the evening.

The morning passed quickly. She had gone in search of Alfie, but he was not in the library. She didn't dare ask anyone else where he might be in case is might arouse suspicion or hard-to-answer questions. She had yet to see Conall and grew more anxious as each hour passed. After lunch, there was a knock on her door and he appeared.

"Alvina will be here shortly to get you ready for this evening. Do you have any questions about what to expect?" he asked, stepping into her room and closing the door behind him.

There were so many questions floating through her head that she seemed unable to grasp only one. Of course, the ever-perceptive Conall sensed her dilemma and sighed. "Do you remember what I told you when we first came here? About controlling your emotions?" She swallowed and nodded. "Tonight will be the most important test of your life. You will see things that will disgust you and may even horrify you. You will see humans being treated poorly, like slaves or pets or even toys, and you cannot react the way your instincts demand. You will have to dance with Unseelie who will sense your human side and wish to feed on or manipulate it. You cannot let them. You *must* remain in control at all times. Do you understand?" He had approached her while he was talking so he was staring right into her eyes at the end of the lecture. He grasped both of her hands in his own.

"I understand," she whispered shakily.

He sighed and soothed her with his calming touch. "We won't be able to touch so familiarly tonight, but I will try to help you as much as I can." He untied the strap at her wrist and pressed it between his palms. His eyes closed in concentration and his hands lit with a faint glow. Several minutes passed, and Lola stared at him in fascination. His lips moved, forming words but not speaking them aloud. Sweat beaded his forehead as the air around them grew heavy and warm. Finally he opened his eyes, and their vivid, shocking, neon green took her breath away. They had never glowed so bright.

He placed the leather tie on the vanity, and its color had changed from brown to a metallic bronze. "I have charmed the leather to hold my power to soothe. It should respond to your own emotions and help calm any fear or panic. Of course, it's not as good as the real thing"—he smirked—"but should help out in a pinch. I would wait to put it on until just before you come downstairs. Its magic will drain depending on how much you use it, or rather, how much you trigger it. Hopefully you will not need it to respond, but I don't want to leave you helpless."

"Thank you, Conall. I will do my best not to let you down," Lola promised.

He reached toward her face and tucked a strand of her hair behind her ear. Her heart skipped a beat. His fingers grazed her cheek and jaw on the way back. "I wish we had more time," he said as he exhaled, leaning closer.

She took a deep breath, inhaling his woodsy scent and taming the butterflies rioting in her stomach. She ached to kiss him. If she just leaned forward a little more, she could press her lips to his.

He dropped his hand from her face and smiled sadly, almost as if his own heart were breaking. He took a step back from her just as a knock sounded from the door and Alvina entered carrying a garment bag. "Excuse us, Sir Conall. I must prepare Lady Ianthe for the bacchanalia," she said briskly.

"Of course, Alvina," he replied. Alvina placed the garment bag across the bed and marched into the bathroom, turning on the faucet to draw a bath for Lola.

"You can do this, my flower. I know you can. You are stronger than you realize, and I will be there with you," he whispered, his fingertips grazing her wrist and sending warmth tingling through her body, all the way down to her toes. "Lady Ianthe, I will see you this evening," he announced, bowing formally before exiting and closing the door behind him.

Lola turned to see Alvina scowling at her from the doorway to the bathroom. "Come now. We don't have all day," she grumped, hustling her into the bath.

Two hours later, Lola felt as if her skin had been scrubbed raw. Alvina must have taken off several layers in the bath, and she was sitting at the vanity staring at herself in awe. Alvina had tugged and tamed her hair into an elegant half up-do of cascading curls, using her humming magic the entire time she worked. Lola's skin glowed and her makeup looked flawless. There was a slight veil of pink to her cheeks and her eyelids sparkled gold. The black eyeliner and mascara made her violet eyes pop. She was amazed at her eyelashes, so full and perfect, like a Maybelline model. Her lips were glossed a shade of deep red, and she had never looked or felt so beautiful. It was like the perfect climax to a makeover montage, and she was slightly giddy anticipating Conall's reaction.

Alvina unzipped the garment bag and Lola released a gasp of surprise. "Beautiful, isn't it?" Alvina said almost wistfully, but that wasn't why Lola had gasped. The dress was a familiar shade of deep purple. She ran her fingers along the fabric. It felt like silk, so airy and light. It was the dress from her first dream with Conall. *How can that be?*

Alvina had her step into the gown then she pulled it up and laced up the back. All the details down to the way it clung to her body, creating curves where she didn't have any, was exactly as she had dreamed. The deep color against her shoulders made her alabaster skin seem to glow, and she looked ethereal. The almost sheer skirt fell below her feet and flowed like water.

"You will wear heels with this dress," Alvina stated, leaving no room for argument. Lola knew flats would not do the dress justice. The shoes were plum, strappy satin things held on by ribbons that crisscrossed and tied around her ankles and up her calves like ballet slippers. She stood and walked over to the mirror. In that moment, she felt and looked every bit of the princess she was. It gave her confidence to face the crowd waiting for her downstairs.

"It's time," Alvina said.

As Alvina left the room, Lola snatched Conall's leather strap from the vanity, wrapped it around her wrist, and tied it. Now, she was ready for whatever the night would bring.

CHAPTER 29

LOLA PAUSED NEAR the end of the hallway; she had been told to wait for the announcer's cue before making her grand entrance. The rest of the guests had already arrived and were awaiting her appearance at the bottom of the stairs. A servant tugged at the sleeve of the announcer, who cleared his throat before his voice rang above the din of the party below. "Lords and ladies of the Unseelie court, I present your Unseelie princess, Lady Ianthe." The crowd held their collective breath as Lola stepped into view. She held her head up high as she carefully strolled into toward the staircase and grasped the railing tight as she descended in her precarious heels. Here and there she paused, searching the crowd for a familiar face. The Unseelie Fae murmured all around her, gossiping, while others stared at her hungrily.

When she reached the bottom of the steps to the main floor, Killian was there to offer her an arm. "You look breathtaking this evening, Lady Ianthe," he whispered in her ear while his eyes never left her chest. "Please allow me to escort you to your father." They walked down the hallway and into the ballroom.

King Corydon sat on his dais at the front of the large room. The ballroom was draped with royal purple and silver fabric, and immense violet bouquets spilled from large flower stands and hung across the ceiling in chains. It was quite a change from the last time she'd been in there. It was dark yet regal and opulent, the epitome of King Corydon. There was a second throne next to the king's, not quite as ornate or large, and it looked as if it were meant for the queen—or the princess, in this case.

As he rose, he plucked her hand from Killian's and held it up for the rest of the crowd to see. Next, he delicately picked up an elaborately jeweled tiara from a pillow sitting to his left. He smiled at Lola like any proud father would as he gently placed the tiara on her head. He then turned toward the crowd. "My daughter, your future queen!" he bellowed, and the crowd roared in applause.

Lola was taken aback for a moment, stunned by all the attention, but quickly schooled her deer-in-headlights look into the regal princess she needed to be. She beamed her pageant smile to the crowd and caught sight of a familiar pair of green eyes in the distance, which put her nerves at ease. Corydon sat down on his throne with a flick of his wrist, indicating that she should do the same. Live music began to play and she glanced around, paying closer attention to the crowd this time, able to see the humans amongst the Fae. The crowd around her began to dance, and her father leaned over to speak with her. "You look every bit like the princess you are tonight, my dear. Have your studies been going well?"

Not accustomed to this polite version of the Unseelie king, she answered him honestly. "Yes, sir. Conall and Alfie have been very helpful. I have learned a lot in such a short time."

"Wonderful! Then you shall be ready to take part in court proceedings starting tomorrow. I am most pleased, my child," he replied.

Her mouth went dry. That was the exact opposite of what she wanted, but it was too late. He was now paying attention to what she assumed was another lord or advisor on his other side.

A tall Fae with silver eyes and straw blond hair approached her. "Lady Ianthe, may I have this dance?" She was unsure of how to respond and glanced quickly at King Corydon, who gave her a slight nod.

"Certainly," she replied with a coy smile, trying to play off her uncertainty as flirting. This was the first in the long procession of Fae men who asked for her to dance. They all held her at a respectful distance, making small talk while they twirled her around the floor. Even the ones with a hungry glint in their eyes didn't seem to bother her. She attributed her steady nerves to Conall's wonderful bracelet, which kept her heart steady and helped her fulfill her role. Most of the night was spent spinning around the dance floor or sitting on the dais, watching the crowd and festivities with a bored expression.

Every so often she would see a Fae pulling a human into a dark corner, smiling as a look of pure terror overtook the human's features. She reminded herself that she had to remain calm. There was nothing she could do for them, and even though it turned her stomach, she continued to act her part.

Halfway through the evening, humans served them a delicious feast with goblets full of ambrosia, the sweet liquid she had tasted before with Conall. She remembered his warning about it being like alcohol and sipped it slowly while others drained their glasses around her. After the meal was eaten and cleared, dancing resumed. The humans in the crowd seemed to be drunk or high, which reminded her of that fateful party night. It seemed as the night wore on, her bacchanalia turned more into the drunken parties she had attended back home. The formalities of dancing were lost as the music turned more drum driven and primal, the beat morphing as drinks flowed, transforming some of the dances from formal into bodies writhing against each other. Lola still maintained every ounce of propriety when dancing and didn't have any of her suitors challenge that, as she was the Unseelie princess and no one wanted to offend the king.

She had only seen glimpses of Conall throughout the evening. She saw him dance with several beautiful Fae women and tried to tamp down her jealousy. She knew he wouldn't ask her to dance because of his position, but how she yearned for it. She was mid dance with yet another Fae male when a chillingly familiar voice spoke over her shoulder.

"May I cut in?"

The Fae she had been dancing with didn't hesitate (and in fact appeared to wince slightly) as he handed her over. "Of course, my lord." Panic swelled in her chest as she closed her eyes and pictured any other Fae than the one she knew now held her hand and swung her into his arms. Her pulse pounded in her ears and her breathing became shallow.

"I told you I would see you again, little one." His voice slithered across her skin. She felt the soothing warmth radiating from Conall's leather strap as she attempted to calm herself as to not draw the attention of anyone else. She opened her eyes and found herself staring into her nightmare. "Ah, there we are." He smiled maliciously down at her, fingering a curl around her face. "Can I tell you how happy I am to see you again? Even more, how excited I was to hear you are exactly who I believed you to be? I'm surprised no one else at that party made the connection, but then again, they had never met your mother." Her eyes widened slightly, her insides trembling. She tried to school her features, remembering that he fed off of her fear. He took her lack of fight as incentive to draw her closer with his other hand on her lower back.

She pushed him away, putting some desperately needed space between them. Drawing on her courage, she smiled. "Can't have any impropriety with the princess, now can we?"

He laughed, causing her stomach to roll. He drew her closer still until he could whisper in her ear, his cheek pressed against hers. "Ahh, little one, you have no need to worry about that. I doubt anyone would judge me for holding my fiancée so closely."

Fiancée.

Her heart stopped, tripped up by that word. When it finally started again, it beat a riot against her chest and she was no longer able to contain her fear. "You must be mistaken. It's…not possible. I'm not your…. I don't have a fiancé. I don't even know who you are." She stopped dancing and tried to wrestle out of his grasp. She was causing a scene and yet no one seemed to step forward to help her. *Where is Conall?*

The music stopped abruptly and King Corydon's voice boomed across the hall, "Ah, Casimir, you made it." Lola turned to stare at her father, who was beaming down at the boy who still held a bruising grip on her wrist.

"Of course, sire. I wouldn't miss my fiancée's bacchanalia for the world." Casimir, the boy with icy blue eyes from Lola's nightmares, smiled toward the king. She kept waiting for Corydon to correct him, and when the words she ached to hear didn't come, she knew things were far worse than she could have possibly imagined.

Chapter 30

CASIMIR DROPPED LOLA'S wrist to approach the king and bow. She couldn't find it in her to make her feet move. She stood in place while the king familiarly smacked Casimir on the back and they turned, discussing his absence and their upcoming nuptials. Bile rose in the back of her throat. She was going to vomit all over the floor in front of everyone. She jumped, startled, as a hand rested on the small of her back until she felt the familiar warmth that radiated from it.

"Now would be a good time to excuse yourself for a moment, Ianthe." She did just that and strode out of the ballroom seeking, refuge in the nearest unoccupied room. Conall was not very long after her, stepping into the room and locking the door.

"Is it true?" she asked, desperately searching his face.

His helplessness gave her the answer she sought before he ever opened his mouth. "I'm afraid so, my flower."

She gulped. "Why didn't you tell me? Why didn't you

say something? How could you not tell me?" she demanded, her voice rising with each question.

"Ianthe, please, lower your voice. I don't want to draw attention to us. I didn't know how to tell you," he stated, like that explained everything.

"This can't be happening. It can't be. It's my nightmare come to life. There is no way—NO WAY I will marry that creep. He…he's…he's the one who…" Her anger faded as panic took root, her chest rising and falling rapidly.

Conall's jaw clenched and he ran his hands down her arms, pushing his calming warmth into her. "Tell me."

She glanced up to his face, hoping with all her might that somehow they could manage to get themselves out of this situation. "He's the one from the party, Conall. He's the one from the woods."

Rage flared in his green eyes. "He's the one who attacked you?" She nodded in confirmation, and he growled in frustration. "Okay, we have to go back out there. I will send you first. Just keep pretending, perhaps feign exhaustion and get excused for the evening. I will sneak back to your room tonight and we will figure this out, I promise." Unable to resist, Conall pulled her toward him and kissed her passionately before setting her in front of the door. "Go first. I will follow later."

She gathered her strength and smoothed her dress, making sure her hair and appearance was all in order before stepping through the door. Thankfully, no one was in the hallway as she snuck back into the ballroom. Casimir was still talking with King Corydon, except now he was seated on her throne. For some reason that fueled her hatred of him, and her fear bled into fury with each step closer. She approached the dais and smiled. "Excuse me, but I believe you are in my seat," she hissed in the syrupy sweet way that lets you know a dragon is sleeping just below the surface.

Corydon chuckled as Casimir stood. "Of course, my love." She clenched her teeth at the term of endearment.

"I'm not anyone's love," she replied coldly.

They both ignored her comment. "Ianthe, let me formally introduce you to my nephew, Casimir."

"It was Prince Casimir until you came along, little one, but no matter. Soon it will be Prince Casimir once again," Casimir added.

"Your nephew? You mean he's my cousin?!" She blanched. *This just keeps getting even worse. Also, ewww.*

"Don't be such a prude, my dear," King Corydon replied while she internally gagged. "Before you came along, I was lacking an heir, so I choose Casimir to take my place should something happen to me. He was most gracious and has trained in the knowledge of the court since he was a young boy. He's been studying the responsibilities of the throne for quite a few years and will continue to do so for at least another century if I have it my way. It's not like I plan on leaving any time soon, but one day he will make a fine king. Of course, I felt he would be the only proper match for you. His knowledge and expertise with our subjects will benefit you and aid their acceptance of you as their future queen."

She swallowed her revulsion. "Thank you, Father, but I'm far too young to get married," she said, trying to reason.

Wrong move.

Corydon leaned forward with a deadly gleam in his eyes. "You dare speak against my decision?" he hissed. "You are in no position to make demands, young lady. You will do as you are told and you will marry Casimir when I tell you to. It's in the best interest of us all."

She wanted to object, but the look on his face told her it would be a grave mistake.

"It's all right, my king. I'm sure she's just worried about being prepared to be a fine queen. Just wait, after a little time with me, she will be chomping at the bit to tie the knot." Casimir's cocky voice oozed charm as he spoke. Luckily, that charm had no effect on Lola.

"I'm afraid time is what we don't have. My sources have reported whisperings among our people. They doubt her as their queen, as my heir, because she is only half Fae. If I believed there was an alternative, a way to bide our time without appearing weak, I would, but this is what I see as fit." Corydon studied her expression carefully before he leaned toward her ear. "You will marry Casimir in three days, or I will break you of your human emotions and ideals myself."

She inhaled sharply, nodding in acknowledgement, and pasted her pageant smile back on her face. "May I be excused, sir? I think all the dancing and excitement has worn me out. I also realize I have a lot of work to do to plan a wedding in that short amount of time." Corydon searched her face with narrowed eyes but seemed to find the answers he was looking for.

"Yes of course," he replied as he casually leaned back in his throne. "I expect you for breakfast with the court in the morning."

"Of course, sir," she replied woodenly as she rose. She threw a fleeting glance at Casimir, who ran his tongue across his sharp teeth and winked suggestively.

"Sweet dreams, my love," he called out as she disappeared into the crowd.

It took every ounce of her strength not to run like her body so desperately wanted to. She calmly climbed the stairs to her room and locked the door behind her, afraid Casimir might want to pay her a late-night visit. She threw off her gown and put on her jeans and t-shirt. There was no way she would sleep in Fae clothes that night. There was a light rap at her door, and she pressed her ear against the wood as she heard Conall's voice. "Ianthe, it's me. Meet me in the library." She waited until his footsteps faded to glance out into the hall. Thankfully, no one was there. The guards must have all still been at the party, and she quickly darted into the library.

"Ianthe, come back to my office please," Alfie's voice called as she entered. She followed it to the back of the library where Alfie and Conall were waiting.

Conall locked the door behind her and scowled. "Are you trying to test his patience? You better hope no one but us sees you in those clothes. He will not let that act of defiance go unpunished."

"I just needed something that would remind me of who I am," she attempted to explain. It seemed to be enough. He nodded like he understood while Alfie looked on sympathetically.

"It's come to my attention that we need a plan fast." Alfie stated. "I wasn't expecting Prince Casimir home so soon, and I was afraid of what might happen when he did arrive. Of course it was exactly how I feared. When did the king say you are to be wed?"

Lola glanced as Conall, who sucked in a deep breath. His face paled and his hands tightly gripped the chair in front of him. Her mouth suddenly went dry. "Three days." A loud crack made her jumped, and she turned to see Conall had snapped the top of chair.

"Damn it!" he roared, pacing wildly. Abruptly, he stopped and faced her. "If I had known—if I had even thought…I would never have brought you here. You have to know that, Ianthe."

She could read the heartbreak in his eyes. "Of course, Conall. I believe you." She then turned toward Alfie. "Now, what are we going to do to stop it?"

CHAPTER 31

W HILE EVERYONE ELSE had been preparing for a party, Alfie had been researching. None of this was out of the norm for Alfie, of course. The only difference was *what* he was researching. He scoured the palace for anything that might help him plan Ianthe's escape. He knew she could abdicate, but she would have to do so publically and then quickly flee. He analyzed Ianthe's and Conall's magic to see how they might use it to aid their escape. He had a plan, but it was a shaky one that may end in all of their deaths or imprisonment and torture. On the other hand, they had to do something before it was too late.

"Here's what I suggest," Alfie began as he carefully explained his plan. It would take an immense acting job on her part and every ounce of her strength to control and manipulate her powers, but he was confident she could do it. It would be harder for Conall to control himself and not let anyone onto the plan. He wanted to wait until the last minute to let Conall in on it, but Casimir's arrival and Conall's protective nature had made that impossible. It wasn't hard to see that Conall had fallen in love with Ianthe, and that was a further complication in the scheme of things. He only hoped Conall could keep his emotions hidden from everyone else.

The next two days seemed to drag by and yet also pass too quickly for her. They needed more time to smooth out the details, but she found no possible way to stall. Any time she attempted to drag her feet, she risked Corydon's wrath, and his patience was running very thin with her lately. The minutes spent with the king and Casimir pretending to be interested in planning her wedding were painfully slow. She acted like every touch Casimir sent her way was wanted and didn't make her want to scrub her skin raw in a scalding hot bath. She acted exactly how an Unseelie princess who was about to get married to a sadistic Unseelie prince should. All the while, she plotted and practiced using her Mara abilities when she was with Alfie or alone.

Unknowingly, King Corydon made things easier for her by insisting that she spend almost every minute she was not wedding planning with Alfie to expedite her education so she would be ready to accept the responsibilities of the throne upon marriage for her official coronation. He wanted to ensure that she was a well-conditioned daughter to make it easier for the court to accept her. On her part, Lola was fully aware of what was expected of her and that if she disappointed him…well, she shuddered to think what he might do to erase her human emotions or "break" her, as he worded it before.

Her time with Casimir was harder to handle. He delighted in seeing how far he could push her until she pushed back, both with his words and his touch, especially in front of her father where she was unable to tell him off. She wasn't sure how Conall made it through those dinners.

She thought for sure someone would read the rage simmering in his gaze and the white-knuckle grip he held on his silverware. She was looking forward to the day when she would be free of the loathsome Casimir once and for all.

She was kept so busy during the day fending off advances from Casimir and "studying" with Alfie that she had only seen Conall in passing or at dinners. She had a feeling this was at Casimir's request, as he must have sensed Conall's fondness toward her. It bothered her as she spent both nights practicing her Mara abilities with Conall in her dreams. She learned to change her appearance at will and mold the scene to her liking. She was growing into her magic the more she learned to control and manipulate her dreams, and of course, it wasn't all work. They were also able to sneak in a few passionate kisses and tender embraces here and there. The night before her wedding was especially sweet.

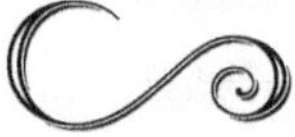

She lay with Conall in a field of violet wildflowers. Her hair appeared in its natural blonde color, something she had been working on. Conall pursed his lips, rolling a lock of hair between his fingers, and frowned.

"I miss the blue," he said with a sigh.

She laughed. "You have a thing against blondes, buddy?"

"Not blondes in particular, but it just doesn't feel like you. You're my violet wildflower," he pouted.

She smiled. "Don't worry, it's only for tonight."

He rolled over and cupped her face. "I have never met anyone like you, Ianthe. You're funny, smart, and gorgeous. You're kind and compassionate. You're everything

I wish I could be but was always afraid to try." His words tugged at her heart, but it felt more like a goodbye than a profession of love. "Ianthe, if anything goes wrong…" His voice was thick, and he paused to gather his emotions. "I just want you to know that I—"

She pressed her fingers against his lips, tears threatening to fall as he tugged on her heartstrings. "Don't say it. Don't you dare say it now—not like this. This is not good-bye, Conall, and I will not have those words said to me like they are one. Save them. Say them when we are free. Our plan will work. It has to."

He nodded, and she removed her fingers only to have him snatch them back and kiss them gently. "Okay, my flower." He kissed her gently again.

"It's time." Lola sighed.

"I'll be with you. Remember to wake up and put on the leather tie I gave you first," Conall whispered, giving her one last peck on the lips. He wouldn't say the words, but she could see the love shining through his eyes in that moment. She knew if their plan didn't work, she wouldn't be the only one to suffer.

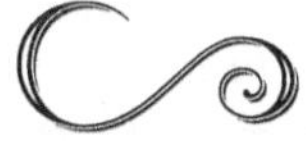

She blinked her eyes open and grabbed Conall's leather strap—freshly charmed and a shimmering metallic bronze—from the bedside table, wrapping it around her wrist. She closed her eyes for a moment and whispered a prayer. "Mom, if you can hear me, please help us. I need you." Lola lay back down and closed her eyes, reaching out to Corydon with her mind.

She saw him appear in the distance. She'd chosen to stage this in the woods by Aunt Grace's house, figuring that was most likely close to where they met. She focused on her appearance. Wavy blonde hair? Check. Blue eyes? Lord, she hoped so. She took several calming breaths, hoping beyond hope that somehow she could make this work. Corydon studied his surroundings cautiously, and she noticed when he recognized where he stood. He started pacing and glancing around as Lola stepped into the moonlight.

"Ayanna?" His voice cracked. "Is it really you?"

"It is," Lola replied, acting the role of her life.

"But...how? I don't understand." He looked baffled.

"You're dreaming, Cor." She sincerely hoped that was the loving nickname her mother would have used with him when they were engaged.

Disappointment flashed across his features. "Of course." His voice sounded like gravel and heartbreak.

She stepped closer to him and he gazed lovingly upon her face.

"You're just as beautiful as I remember."

She smiled at him, imagining what her mom must have seen to fall in love with him.

He cautiously reached a hand to her face and she fought her instinct to back away, instead pretending it was Conall's hand caressing her. "You're really here."

Just as suddenly as his loving adoration appeared, it shifted into something much darker and his features contorted in anger. His loving caress became a bruising grip on her face. "You left me," he spat.

"Cor, let me go. You're hurting me," she pleaded.

"I gave you EVERYTHING! And you left me!" he

roared.

She winced. If she hadn't been wearing Conall's strap on her wrist, she was sure she wouldn't have been able to contain her panic. Instead the calm helped her focus and direct her emotions. She yanked free of his grip and took a step back. "You want to know why?! This is why! You changed. Being the Unseelie king changed you." She imagined what it must have felt like to be her mother, in love with a man who turned cruel over time, finding out she was pregnant with his child. "There was no way I could bring a child into the Unseelie court after seeing what it did to you." The moment those words left her lips, the rightness of them resonated deep within her bones. She knew her mother had left to save her.

Corydon's rage twisted features softened. "How could you not tell me about her?"

She thought for a moment, imagining what it must have been like for her mom. She remembered back to the dream where she'd talked to her mom. "I didn't want her to be an Unseelie. I didn't want her to lose her humanity. I knew if you found out, you wouldn't have let either of us go."

"You're right about that," he hissed. Man, this guy was all over the place. She treaded lightly, seeking to appease his anger and reason with him, needing to focus if her plan was going to work.

"I'm sorry, Cor. You know I loved you, but when I left, you were no longer the man I had fallen in love with. I had to do what was best for Ianthe." She reached forward to lovingly caress his cheek as her mother must have done a thousand times. She knew it would only work if she could present this as his idea, not hers. "Now that you've met our daughter, what do you think?"

"She is far from what an Unseelie princess should be,"

he replied with a snort.

Lola sighed, fearing there was no way the plan would work.

He studied her reaction closely. "But she looks just like you. Sometimes it's painful to look at her. It reminds me how much I loved you and how much it hurt me when you left." She held her hand still against his cheek and clearly saw the pain behind his eyes. "She daydreams just like you and has a fiery spirit, but she's too fragile...too human."

She took a deep breath, praying this would work and she wouldn't anger him again. "That's because she is half human. You know it will be her weakness if she becomes queen. The Seelie court will sense her humanity and use it to their advantage." She let her hand drop from his face.

"I know." He sighed. Hope spread like a wildfire through her veins.

"Sometimes being king means making sacrifices, and so does being a parent. We sacrifice for those we love. I know you knew that once upon a time, and I know despite all of your attempts to act the way an Unseelie king should, the man I loved is still under there somewhere. You know what's best for your people may not be what's best for you or for Ianthe." She knew she was pressing her luck, but she had to make sure he was swayed enough to let her go. Corydon looked at the grass and contemplated what she'd said. She felt the fatigue of using her Mara abilities increasing, and a small strand of her blonde hair turned blue. She struggled to hide it before he noticed. She was running out of time.

"I must leave now. Our time is up. Take care of our little Ianthe for me." She pecked his cheek before turning to leave. He looked defeated for a moment, but then seemed to gather himself. "Protect her and keep her safe.

Goodbye, Cor." Lola quickly stepped back into the darkness before he could stop her.

CHAPTER 32

LOLA SLEPT THE rest of the night without dreaming, having exhausted herself and her magic. She blinked her eyes open as the sun streamed in through her window. One look at her armoire and the dress hanging there reminded her it was supposed to be her wedding day, the day she would marry Casimir. *Of course, there is no way in hell that wedding will ever happen if I can help it. Alfie's plan has to work. There's no other option. Hell, death may even be preferable to marrying Casimir.* She shuddered at the thought of what he would do to her, what he would expect on their wedding night, how he would treat her as his wife. She carefully selected her outfit from the closet for breakfast, a long flowing skirt that would hide her jeans underneath. She sighed knowing there was no way her t-shirt would make it. She picked up the piece of fabric that matched her skirt and wrapped it around her bodice twice in a crisscross manner as she had seen some of the other Fae wearing around the palace. She pulled the fabric so it covered as much of her skin as possible.

She ran a brush through her hair, humming like she had heard Alvina do. It didn't look nearly as good as when Alvina did it, but she was starting to get the hang of it. She repeated the humming with the makeup brush, running it across her skin. She picked out the most practical sandals, made sure Conall's strap was tied around her wrist, and caressed it with a smile upon her lips as she thought about their shared dream the previous night. Finally she took a deep breath and calmed her racing heart before opening her door.

Conall was leaning against the wall in the same casual pose he'd assumed that first night she saw him against the tall oak. She smiled, suddenly feeling shy. "Hi."

He smiled in return. "You look nice. You ready for this?" She took a deep breath and nodded as he escorted her down to the dining hall. "Remember, as soon as you abdicate, you must leave while the chaos has everyone distracted. Alfie has horses ready for us outside, and I will escort you back to your Aunt Grace's house. She has someone ready to help conceal you."

Lola stopped short. "But what about you? Will you be going with me? What will happen to you after I get away?" He looked away and wouldn't meet her eyes. The hesitation told her all she needed to know. "No, Conall. You cannot risk yourself just to save me. I won't allow it."

"Don't worry, my flower. I have everything in place. We will both be fine." He lied so smoothly that it only gave her slight pause before she nodded as he slowed to walk behind her as they entered the dining hall.

The room was brimming with lords and ladies of the Fae court, far more than had joined them for breakfast any of the other days she had been there, but then again, with the oncoming wedding, she could see why. "Ahh, there's my daughter now," King Corydon's voice boomed across the hall. When she looked toward him, he appeared as he did every day. Only someone who knew how to read his closely guarded emotions could see the slight sadness in his eyes as she approached.

She took her seat next to Casimir, as was expected of her. He leaned forward and whispered in her ear, "Good morning, little one." His tongue snaked out and licked her ear, causing her to shudder in repulsion. "I cannot wait to taste you tonight when you become my wife. I can assure you that no one will interrupt us this time." He pulled back and hungrily gazed upon her. Knowing her fear set him off, she mustered her anger and hatred instead. She glared daggers in his direction while he chuckled and settled back into his chair.

Lola picked at the food in front of her. Sneaking glances around the room and controlling her growing nerves, she steeled her resolve. She noticed Conall approach the king and whisper something in his ear. The king nodded and Conall met her inquisitive gaze with a slight nod before leaving the room. *Well, it's now or never.*

She rose from her seat, her chair scraping against the floor loudly. The court quieted, not sure what to make of her actions. Casimir narrowed his eyes upon her and the king turned his head her way. "Is there something you need, Ianthe?" Corydon asked.

She took a deep breath. "Yes, Father." She stood and approached the king at the head of the table. His lips tightened, indicating that her behavior was not what he was expecting and could bring down his wrath. His eyes narrowed as she raised her head and turned to face the court. "Lords and ladies of the court," she began. Silence greeted her as her words carried across the room. "King Corydon,

I—" She paused to clear her throat and gather her courage. In a voice that rang like a bell, she then called out, "I abdicate my throne as princess to the Unseelie Court." Gasps and murmurs rang out from the crowd. Casimir looked ready to kill. She risked a glance at her father, hoping this would work, praying his dream of her mother had been enough. He clenched his fists against the table but looked like he was waging an emotional war inside his head.

Casimir stood abruptly, his chair falling to the floor with a loud clang. "Unacceptable!" he boomed. "She does not know what she's saying!" The murmurs from the court grew to a clamor.

"Enough!" King Corydon's voice roared above the din, instantly silencing the room. Lola took a sharp intake of air at the sound and rubbed the strap around her wrist. "Leave. All of you. I wish to speak to my daughter alone." The court quickly and quietly fled the room, all except Casimir. The king turned toward him. "Casimir, that means you too."

"But sir, the wedding…and I—"

"Get out!"

Lola hadn't thought it was possible for him to yell any louder than he had, but he proved her wrong, sending chills down to her bones. This wasn't part of the plan. She was supposed to be able to sneak out during the chaos and confusion of her announcement, not be stuck alone with the king who had threatened to break her of her humanity.

"Do you have any idea what you've done?!" he growled, slamming his fist against the table. Goblets fell over and plates clattered with the force.

Lola gulped but held her head high. "Yes, as a matter of fact, I do. You left me no choice, *Father*. Such an interesting word father is. While you may be my biological father, you have never once cared for me as a father should. If you loved me at all, you would want what's best for me."

"What's best for you?" Corydon roared. "Being queen is what's best for you!"

"You know it's not. You know in your heart it's not. It's not what's best for me, and it's certainly not what's best for the Unseelie. They will never truly accept me as their queen with me being a half-breed. I don't have the stomach for it, and you know it. I don't want to be their queen, and that alone makes me unfit for the job."

His rage cooled to a simmer. "I could make you, you know. I could strip you of your humanity and you would make a fine queen."

It's now or never. "You could, but that's not what Mom wanted. She took me away because she wanted me to be human and to cherish my humanity."

His eyes widened. "How do you know?"

"Because she told me in a dream," she answered truthfully.

A ghost of a smile graced his lips. "Of course she did." He remained silent for a few minutes, stewing over what she had said, and then Conall burst into the room.

"Ianthe!" he gasped, short of breath. "I thought…I was…"

"Ah, Conall, just in time." King Corydon smiled maliciously. "Would you please take my dear daughter to the dungeon?"

Conall blanched, obviously conflicted over the orders, and Corydon sensed his hesitation. "Need I remind you that to refuse my order would be considered an act of treason?" He quirked an eyebrow at him. "You remember what we do to traitors, don't you?" Conall winced.

"Conall," Lola pleaded. "Just take me to the dungeon. It's okay."

"I suggest you do as the lady tells you," Corydon stated.

Conall sighed and reached for her, gently guiding her out of the room. "What happened?"

She tried to tell him but when they turned the corner, he roughly grabbed her wrists. "I'm sorry, my love, but we have to make them believe," he whispered in her hair as he yanked her arms behind her.

Peeking over her shoulder, she saw that the entire court had gathered in the great room to see what would happen to her. She stared down at the floor while Conall pretended to roughly lead her to the dungeon. As he took her through halls she had not seen yet, she began to second-guess their plan. Where had they gone wrong? When they didn't see any more Fae in the corridors, he loosened his hold on her as he opened a heavy wooden door. "I really hate to bring you down here, but I don't see any other choice at this moment." He looked apologetically into her eyes. She understood. She wouldn't want him to be tried for treason, and she would sacrifice herself in a heartbeat if it meant saving him.

"It's okay, Conall, really," she said softly, trying to reassure him, but he only grew more conflicted as they stepped through the door. He guided her in front of him down a dimly lit staircase of stone. It reminded her of the dungeon you would see in a medieval castle, and she hoped it was not like the ones she had seen in some movies and shows. To her horror, everything seemed to be spot on. There were chains dangling from the walls with shackles. In some places, the stone floor was stained a dark reddish brown, and she shivered at the thought of who had suffered there. They passed cages holding strange Fae creatures inside, and an emaciated man who may have already been dead was shackled to one wall. She glanced up to see a greasy guard smirk at her and run his tongue across his sharp teeth. Conall led her to a cell away from the other prisoners and the guards, perhaps to shield her from the horrors of that place.

"I will get you out of this, my flower. I promise," he swore as they approached her cell. He kissed her passionately and roughly after they stepped into the stone-walled cell. "Be strong. I will find Alfie and we *will* figure this out." The metal door clanged behind him as Ianthe studied the cold, damp walls of her cell. She took a deep breath. She had to be strong and find a way out of this mess. She didn't think Conall would be able to last long while she was down here. Sooner or later, he would try to rescue her or do something that would get him into hot water with the king.

CHAPTER 33

HER LIPS STILL tingling from his kiss, Lola took Conall's words to heart. She would not be a weeping damsel in distress. She looked around the dungeon and met the predatory gaze of the guards. The door clanged open and Casimir stepped through. She backed away from the bars of her cell as he approached.

"You think you can outsmart me, little one?" he seethed. "This is even better than I hoped. Perhaps as punishment for your insubordination, the king will give you to me as a slave. I won't even have to marry you to be prince now." He grinned, flashing his sharp teeth, and looked her over hungrily as he stepped forward and wrapped his hands around the bars, leaning in toward her as far as they would allow. "Make no mistake, *Princess*, you will be mine." He turned on his heels and stormed back out of the dungeon. She wondered why she'd ever thought this plan would work. She had doomed them all.

Growing weary, she tried to make herself comfortable. Glad to have her jeans underneath, she removed her long skirt, placing it on the floor, and lay down on it, drifting off to sleep. She longed to go see Aunt Grace but didn't want to explain the situation and worry her, so she called to Conall instead, hoping perhaps he may be napping as well, but she couldn't reach him.

She yawned and opened her eyes to find herself in the woods by Aunt Grace's house. "My sweet Ianthe," her mother's sweet voice whispered on the breeze. "I'm so proud of you. You did well today."

"Obviously not well enough," Ianthe responded, letting some of her self-pity seep in.

"Nonsense. All will be fine, you'll see. Just remember everything I told you the last time we spoke. Who we are is not predetermined. It's about the choices we make. The same can be said about the Fae—not all Fae are bad, not even all Unseelie. You, my dear, are proof of that."

She closed her eyes, unsure if her dream was merely her mind trying to reassure her or something magical and impossible. "I love you, Mom."

"I love you too, my violet flower, my sweet Ianthe."

The clang of the dungeon door woke her. As a hooded figure approached, she scooted back against the wall, afraid it may be Casimir, but then again, he probably wouldn't disguise himself. The mysterious person neared her cell and took out a key. "Lady Ianthe, you must go now."

"Alfie? Oh my goodness! Alfie!"

"Shhh! Quickly now." He placed the key in the door and released her.

"Where are the guards?" she asked.

"They are receiving orders from the first in command." Alfie winked. Conall must have given them this opportunity to escape. "Come now, our horses await." He led her up the stairs, making sure they went unseen as they snuck through the empty kitchen and out the doors.

Right outside, two horses were saddled and waiting. Alfie helped her onto one then carefully mounted the other.

"What about Conall?"

Alfie carefully avoided her gaze and question. "We must leave now, before someone notices you are gone. He will follow." With that answer he turned and reined his horse into a full gallop, fleeing the castle walls. Lola had no choice but to do the same if she didn't want to be left behind. They rode out of the town as fast as they could.

Lola didn't know how far they would have to travel because she had been unconscious during her previous trip from the gate. Alfie slowed his horse to a canter and she pulled alongside him. "Alfie, how did you get the key to my cell?"

He chuckled. "Oh, that was easy. It was given to me."

"By whom?"

"By your father."

"My *father*? King Corydon?"

He laughed again. "Who else would be your father dear?"

She bit down her immediate response, almost startled by the homesickness she felt at that moment for the man she'd believed to be her father for her whole life. "But why would Corydon give you the key?"

"Ah. That, my dear, is a very interesting story. He visited me not long after you were taken to the dungeon and told me about a most vivid dream he had where your mother came to visit him." He winked. "It seems your words may have stirred something inside of him, and he found himself wondering how he might be able to release you without angering the court.

"Since you abdicated the throne publicly, he could not let the act go unpunished. I merely suggested that your punishment be exile to the human realm. Many Fae find this punishment worse than death, so it seemed like it might just work. He gave me the key and told me to get you out of Fae before he made his announcement, in case anyone decided to take your punishment into their own hands."

She took a while to consider his words and what they might mean. She glanced up at the bright moon. Perhaps there was a small sliver of love still in Corydon's heart, after all. She smiled until she remembered that they were missing a companion. "Alfie, what about Conall?" No sooner had the words left her lips than they heard a horse in the distance.

"Hopefully that will be him now, but we should conceal ourselves just in case," he suggested. They pulled their horses toward a patch of dense forest and kept them as still as possible. When the figure approached, she breathed a sigh of relief as she saw the rider's hair was long and pulled back into a ponytail instead of short and spiky.

"Conall?" she whispered.

"It's me." His honeyed voice made her exhale in relief.

"Thank goodness! Are you okay?"

"Yes, my flower, but we must make haste."

The three of them pressed their horses to move as quickly as they could through the dense wood until they reached the white sycamore archway. Alfie took the lead. Lola's skin tingled as she passed through, but it was much easier this time. Once they had crossed, they stopped for a moment so Conall could make sure Lola was okay. He jumped off his horse and ran over to her, grabbing her in his arms. "I was so worried when I heard the commotion in the dining hall, and I didn't know what to do when the king ordered me to take you to the dungeon. I wouldn't be able to live with myself if something happened to you." He kissed her hair then cupped her face, pressing his lips to hers. She sighed happily and gazed adoringly into his bright green eyes. "Ianthe, I lo—"

A twig snapped to their left and Conall turned, pushing her behind him and drawing his sword in one smooth motion.

"Tsk, tsk, tsk. What would the king have to say about this, Conall?" Casimir stepped out from behind a tree. "And you, little one, here I thought you just weren't affected by our Fae charms. Your feelings for him will make this that much sweeter." He smiled maliciously, drawing his own sword.

"Ianthe, you must go now," Conall ordered.

"I will not leave you."

"You must. Mount your horse. Alfie, lead her home please. Be safe, my flower." He caressed her wrist before making sure she mounted her horse.

Sword drawn, Casimir stood watching the exchange with a hint of amusement. "Don't worry, little one, I'll take care of your boy," he sneered before lunging toward Conall, their swords clashing.

CHAPTER 34

LOLA JUMPED AT the sound of the striking swords, which spooked her horse, causing it to race off through the woods with Alfie close behind. As soon as she managed to control her horse, she pulled it to a halt.

"Milady, we must keep going," Alfie implored.

"I cannot leave him behind. I can't let him be hurt because of me." She turned her horse.

"Please, milady. He would want you to be safe!" Realizing she would not change her mind, Alfie sighed in resignation and turned his horse to follow her.

She heard the sounds of the fight—the grunts of effort mixing with the clangor of metal against metal—before she approached. She dismounted her horse as quickly as possible and raced to get closer on foot so she would not distract Conall.

"When I finish with you, I will hunt down your *little flower* and feast on her flesh."

"You will not touch her!" Conall roared back, striking with his sword, which Casimir blocked. Ianthe crept closer, focusing more on the fight than her footsteps.

Snap! That was all it took—a split second and a large twig snapping—for Conall to whip his head in her direction. She watched, horrified as Casimir used the distraction to his advantage and swung the blade of his sword across Conall's chest.

"NOOO!" she screamed, racing toward them. Conall fell to his knees and collapsed on the forest floor. She slid on her knees beside him, assessing the damage and putting pressure on the wound to staunch the bleeding. "No, no, no, no, no. This can't be real." There was so much blood. She heard Casimir chuckle in the distance and swung her head in his direction, fire blazing in her eyes. "You! You did this!"

"Of course I did." He scoffed. "What did you expect?"

She reached down to push herself up and grabbed a grapefruit-sized jagged rock from the forest floor. She clenched it in her fist, approaching Casimir in her fury.

"And just what do you intend to do about it, little one? Are you here to kiss and make up? Perhaps you need a new boyfriend to replace your dying one?" he taunted.

His words broke something in her. She rushed toward him at full speed and brought the rock down on the side of his head. She struck him once and he staggered back. Determined, she hurled the rock at his head with all her might. It struck his left temple with a sickening thud and he crumpled to the ground. She walked over to assess the damage. Blood flowed steadily from the wound, but his chest rose and fell, so she knew he was still alive. She glanced over at where Conall lay, Alfie crouching next to him and tending to his wounds. She took a deep, cleansing breath and forced her mind into a meditative state, calling upon her Mara powers to help her end this once and for all.

She stood in the front yard of the party house with the bass thumping through the ground. This time she had nothing to fear. She knew she was in control. She stepped into the party, seeking him out for a change. She spotted him immediately, and his icy blue eyes swirled with excitement. He licked his sharp teeth in anticipation and she turned, making her way through the crowd and down the hall. She glanced back to make sure he was following her. She wanted to make him think she was his prey when she was actually the one hunting him. Of course he fell for it, tracking her movements and slithering through the crowd behind her.

She paused and yanked a cup out of a partygoer's hand, draining the amber liquid that burned down her throat. "Hey!" he exclaimed, but quickly relented when she smiled flirtatiously at him. He took that as an invitation to approach her but was quickly yanked away from behind.

"Mine!" Casimir hissed. The boy threw his hands up and backed away as if to say she was all his. Ha! Like she was his to give away in the first place. "What game are we playing this time, little one?" He quirked his eyebrow and she giggled, encouraging him to give chase.

She darted down the hall and into a bedroom. This was her dream to control, not his.

Casimir slid into the room seconds after her and closed the door, clicking the lock into place. He smiled seductively. "I didn't know you wanted to play. Such a treat you're turning out to be. I can't wait to taste you again." He stalked closer to her with every step, and she backed away toward the bed. "We can pretend this is our wedding night. I had so many plans, and I intend to put them into action right now." He reached for her, gripping her waist. He inhaled her scent and licked the slender column of her neck. She shuddered, trying not to vomit, and he took it as an encouraging shiver. "Mmm...you are delicious, little one."

He shoved her onto the bed and she waited for him to climb on top of her. The minute he did, she used every ounce of her strength to flip him over and straddled him.

"Oooo, I do love a woman on top." He leered suggestively. She reached across him toward the head of the bed and he groaned. She pulled out shackles and secured his wrists in place. "Kinky—I like it." She ignored him and jumped off to secure his ankles in similar shackles. "And what will you do with me now, little one?"

She smiled. He probably thought this was the greatest dream he'd ever had. She pulled a switchblade from her pocket and flipped it open with a satisfying snap. Casimir's half-lidded eyes snapped wide, eyeing her and the knife with increasing concern.

"Wh-What are you are doing?" She just smiled sweetly. Now it was his turn to be afraid. "Why doesn't my magic work?" He thrashed against his shackles. His fear washed over her like a delicious drug and she almost moaned, wondering if this was what it was like to be a true Mara.

"Tsk, tsk, tsk," she said, throwing his words back at him. "You're not the one in control here—I am." She climbed onto the bed and straddled him again, looking at him with an expression of feigned concern. "What's wrong? You don't like my new game? I was thinking it was time for me to be the hunter and you to be the prey." She watched his Adam's apple bob up and down as he gulped.

It was the first time she had ever seen Casimir actually look afraid. She traced the knife across his chest and cut open his shirt. He hissed when the cold blade came in contact with his skin, and she smiled. "Here's the deal. You are going to let me, Alfie, and Conall go and never come after us again." She dug the knife in, making the first cut, and watched as blood pooled underneath the blade.

"Fuck!" Casimir yelped. She didn't want to admit how much his cries fueled her.

"Hurts, doesn't it?" she sneered. "Just think, I could do this all night, every night. Can you imagine? Every. Single. Night." She dragged the blade lightly up to his cheek and pressed it into his skin. Casimir hissed through clenched teeth. "See, Cas, I don't have a problem with visiting you every night and being the one in control—and I will be in control, every...single...time." She made a fine cut down his cheek applying pressure with each word. "I never wanted to play this game with you. I never wanted anything to do with you. If there were a way I could have avoided all of this, I would have taken it, but you've left me no choice, so I will play. I will haunt your dreams and turn them into your worst nightmares. So, what do you say? Will you finally let me go?" She scraped the knife on his throat, digging it lightly into his skin and leaving a trail of blood, then she pressed the blade against his Adam's apple when he swallowed.

"Fine," he whispered. The heady power made her head spin. She could end this right then, could watch the blood and life drain from his body. For a few moments, she struggled internally, drawn to her newfound sense of power.

"What's that? I couldn't hear you." She increased the pressure of the blade, enjoying his discomfort too much.

"Fine!" he yelled. "Fine. I will let you go, little one. As for your boy and Alfie, that is not up to me—that is up to the king."

"And you are the future king, so please be sure my father chooses wisely. I have no problem visiting you both every night." She flashed her megawatt pageant smile, and he winced. She climbed off of him and leaned over to whisper in his ear. "Oh, and so help me God, if Conall does not make it, I'll ensure your nightmares will make you wish I had killed you when I had the chance." She stared him straight in the eye so he would see she was deadly serious. Then she thrust the blade down into the center of his right hand, pinning it to the mattress. He screamed. The sound made her feel high, and she inhaled deeply, buzzing until she realized she was feeding off his pain. It seemed she truly was part Unseelie.

Disgusted with herself, she turned and left. The second she stepped out of the room, she braced herself against the wall. Her legs shook and she had no clue how she had been able to pull that off, but she thought she deserved an Oscar for her performance.

Lola blinked her eyes open. She was still sitting next to an unconscious Casimir. She turned, searching for Alfie and Conall, and pulled herself up, stumbling toward them. "Alfie! How is he?"

Alfie's face looked grim. "Not so good, milady. I need to take him back to the Fae realm. We have medicines and healers there that can save him, but if we don't get him there soon, I'm afraid it will be too late."

"Okay, I will follow behind," she replied, rushing to

grab her horse.

"Ianthe, I'm afraid you can't," he called after her, stopping her in her tracks.

"What do you mean, I *can't*?" she rasped.

"Part of being exiled is that you cannot return to the Fae realm without penalty of execution," he explained.

She gasped.

"No time to waste, milady. I must take him now. It will give him comfort to know I sent you on to your aunt's house where you will be safe."

Her hands trembled as she approached Conall. There was so much blood on his clothes. She caressed his check tenderly and bent to kiss his lips. "Conall, you must fight, you hear me. I cannot lose you now. Fight with everything you have," she whispered against his skin. A tear escaped and ran down her cheek. His hand wiped it away and she opened her eyes to see his brilliant green ones staring back at her. "Conall, I lo—"

"A a wise girl once told me those words should never be used as a goodbye," he rasped, interrupting her.

She smiled, hearing her words from their shared dream used against her. She helped Alfie hoist a semi-conscious Conall onto his horse then Alfie climbed on behind him and took the horse's reins. They used a rope from the saddle to tie Conall to Alfie in a sitting position, so even if he slumped over during the ride, he would not fall.

"Save him, Alfie. *Please.*"

Alfie drew the reins and urged the horse into a gallop through the white sycamore archway. Lola wanted to collapse right there under the stars, but Casimir was still unconscious not so far away, and she didn't feel it was wise. She somehow found the strength to mount her horse. "Take me home," she whispered in its ear, hoping it knew the way because, she did not. She wrapped her arms around its neck, sobbing into its mane as they galloped into the night.

Chapter 35

S HE DIDN'T KNOW how she made it back to her aunt's house; perhaps the horse knew the way after all, or perhaps it was her mother helping to keep her safe. The horse stopped in the clearing and she practically fell off of him. She stroked his muzzle gently to thank him and he turned, taking off for what she assumed to be the Fae realm. She stumbled up the porch steps and opened the door, which was thankfully unlocked. "Aunt Grace?" she called, climbing the stairs.

She stepped onto the landing as Grace opened her bedroom door. "Lola? Lola!" She rushed forward just as Lola collapsed into a sobbing heap on the floor. Grace gathered her in her arms and carried her to bed where she rocked her to sleep, rubbing her back and hair and whispering soothing words in her ear. Eventually Lola's crying stopped when exhaustion overtook her.

She stood in their special meeting place by the tall oak, but there was no Conall. She knew she was dreaming, but she still had hoped he would be there. She imagined herself at Conall's house, but after a thorough search of his cottage, she still did not find him. She called for him endlessly, begging, pleading with anyone who may hear to help her find him, but she was greeted with nothing but silence. Finally, she climbed onto his bed, which still carried his scent, and buried herself in his sheets, praying he would be okay.

She woke the next morning alone in her bed at Aunt Grace's house. She sighed, feeling dazed to be home. She sent a quick prayer to the heavens for Conall and got up. When she ventured downstairs, she found Grace making breakfast. "Oh Lola, good morning, sweetheart." Aunt Grace greeted her, putting down her spatula and wrapping her in a tight hug.

"Aunt Grace…could you please call me Ianthe instead of Lola?" she asked. She had decided her Fae magic was what had saved her in the end, so maybe she should start embracing that part of her. Also, the name now reminded her of her mother, and of Conall. Her heart ached.

"Of course, Ianthe." Grace smiled. It felt right being called by the name her mom and Conall both loved so much. It almost made her feel like they were there with her.

Over breakfast, she told Grace everything that had happened since the first night she saw Conall outside her window. She told her all about meeting her father, her bacchanalia, the other Fae, and especially Conall. When she got to the events of the previous night, she choked down a sob thinking of his injury, but Grace reassured her that he would be fine. There were Fae healers that could heal even the most deadly wounds with magic. Ianthe told her about her dream and how she couldn't find Conall when she should have been able to. Grace tried to reassure her that things would be fine, but she still worried.

Grace spent most of the morning trying to distract her with chores and the gorgeous, demon-hunting Winchester brothers, but all she could think about was Conall. Later that afternoon, Grace's voice broke through her cloud of gloom. "You know, I've been thinking, and I have a theory about why you couldn't find Conall in your dreams last night. I think you are able to communicate through your dreams with other Fae only when you're in the same realm. Think about it: you first dreamed with Conall when he was here outside the house, and the other times you dreamed with him were when you were both in the Fae realm. When he went away for those few weeks, you didn't share any dreams."

It did make some sense. "But then why could I share dreams with you when I was in Fae and you were here?"

"Perhaps since I'm human it's easier than with other Fae, or maybe it has something to do with the magic in our bloodline that gives us the gift of Sight. Or, perhaps if you were full-blooded Fae you could share dreams across realms with other Fae, but I'm pretty sure that's the reason why."

Ianthe thought it over carefully. "I think you might be right." She sighed. "How am I supposed to know he's okay? How will I ever be okay if he…if he—" Her voice broke. She couldn't even say the word for fear it might be true.

Grace hugged her. "We'll find a way, honey. We'll find a way."

The days dragged by with no word of Conall's health. Ianthe was beginning to go crazy with worry to the point of debating risking penalty of execution to sneak back into Fae. Of course, that was if she could even find the way to the gateway on her own. Finally, one morning she opened the door to gather blackberries and Alfie stood on Grace's porch. "Alfie!" she shrieked, dropping the basket and wrapping her arms around him. After a few moments, she released him. "Come in, come in please."

"What's all the commotion?" Grace asked, appearing over her shoulder. "Oh, we have a visitor."

Ianthe introduced them then Grace led the way into the kitchen for breakfast. Before they could sit, Ianthe grasped Alfie's hands. "You must tell me about Conall—is he okay?"

Alfie smiled reassuringly at her. "Yes, milady, he is healing well. The cut was deep and he had lost much blood by the time I got him to his house that evening. I was afraid to travel farther into town with him. It was touch and go for a while, but luckily he had the proper salves and potions to help him heal. The next day the king sent a healer to check on him and take over his care, and I was ordered back to the castle."

Ianthe was disappointed with this explanation. *If Conall is all right, why isn't he here? Why is Alfie here instead?* Grace and Alfie talked over breakfast while Ianthe got lost in her thoughts.

"Ianthe?"

She glanced up to see Aunt Grace and Alfie looking at her with concerned expressions. "I'm sorry, what was that?"

Grace smiled at her softly, patting her arm. "It's okay dear."

"Alfie, when do you think I will see Conall?"

He looked uncomfortable with the question. "I'm not quite sure, milady."

She inhaled sharply. "Did Casimir do something?"

"Oh no, nothing like that. Casimir has actually been distant and chooses to ignore both of us. What I mean is that he's still healing and then His Majesty has ordered him to travel to the Seelie court for negotiations. I don't know when he will be able to sneak away."

Her heart sank. Why didn't Conall want to be with her? She thought he loved her, but he was choosing to stay in the Fae realm.

Alfie looked on sympathetically. "I'm sorry, Princess. I wish I had better news to bring you."

"It's okay. Please let him know I miss him more than words can say."

"Of course. I must be going now. I'm afraid my time is up and if the king has to send someone for me, the consequences will not be pleasant."

"Please, come visit us again," Grace called as Ianthe escorted Alfie to the door.

"I'm afraid I will not be able to visit again, Princess. I have used all of the king's good favors and graces with my last few excursions."

"I understand, Alfie. It was an honor to meet you and I wish you happiness in your future. Please take care of yourself." She pecked him on the cheek and hugged him tightly.

He was blushing when she released him. "Of course, Lady Ianthe. Take care of yourself as well, and I will watch over Conall for you." He stepped off the porch and into the clearing, turned around, and waved once before disappearing into the woods. She sighed, wondering if she would ever see him or Conall again.

The summer days passed in a blur and Grace proved to be the mother figure Ianthe had always yearned for. Grace's love was the perfect remedy for her broken heart. Ianthe had no dreams with Conall, and even though she looked every night before she went to bed, she never saw his masculine frame leaning against the great oak. Her therapist called and checked in on her, and she was surprised when he asked about her sobriety. All that almost felt like a lifetime ago, and she happily reported that she had been doing well and hadn't thought about using since the first few days after she arrived. Of course, he found that hard to believe, but she couldn't exactly explain to him that her time in the Fae realm had cured her of such things.

Soon her summer was over and it was time to leave. Her father came to pick her up, and their relationship was still as strained as ever, especially when he voiced his opinion of her name change and refused to call her anything other than Lola. Saying goodbye to Aunt Grace was difficult, but she managed through her tears. They had made a pact to share dreams at least once a week to keep in touch, and Grace was already coordinating with her dad for her to visit over her winter break from school.

While her heart still ached for Conall, she was glad for everything she had experienced that summer. She knew who she was now. She was Ianthe, a half-blood Unseelie Fae princess, a Mara, her mother's daughter. She was the one in control of her fate. Her only regret was not being able to tell Conall those three little words, so she whispered them on a breeze, hoping there might be just a little magic left in the world to carry them to him. She climbed into the car and closed the door on that chapter of her life.

EPILOGUE

CONALL AWOKE WITH a start to find himself in his cabin. His body ached and his chest burned. He glanced down to see blood-soaked bandages around his chest and he remembered the fight with Casimir. *What happened to Ianthe?* He gathered his strength and sat up, trying to get up from the bed.

"I wouldn't do that if I were you." Alfie's voice rang out from a corner of his room.

"Alfie! Where is Ianthe?" he asked, panicking.

"Calm yourself, Conall. She is fine. She's a strong and determined girl. It took quite some arguing on my part for her to allow me to return with you. She's safe now at her aunt's house, I'm sure."

"What happened?" he asked, trying to put together the pieces of the previous night.

"Well, Casimir struck a mighty blow upon you. By the time I could reach you to tend to your wounds, Ianthe was attacking Casimir. She knocked him out after striking his head twice with a rock, I believe. While I was patching you up the best that I could, I can only assume she paid Casimir a little visit in his unconscious dreams as I saw she was meditating. When she returned to your side, I told her I must bring you back to the Fae realm to heal you, but she could not go with us. She was most brokenhearted, I assure you, and had it not been upon the penalty of death, I think she would have come back with us. I couldn't allow that and knew you wouldn't want that either, so I sent her on to her aunt's house. I was assured that she made it safely when her horse calmly returned. I'm positive she's most anxious to hear about you," Alfie explained.

"Well this wasn't how we planned things, but the important thing is that she is safe." Their plan had been for him to run away with her. He sighed and the movement of his chest sent a sharp stab of pain through him. He clenched his jaw.

"Here, drink some of this and rest. You will do her no good in this state," Alfie ordered, handing him an herbal potion. Conall sipped the bitter tea down and drifted back to sleep.

The next few days were a bit hazy. He knew a healer—rough, but extremely efficient—had been sent to tend to him, and he was glad for her help. Alfie returned to the castle once the healer arrived, by order of the king, he was sure. Finally, after three days, the deep wounds seemed to have sealed shut, leaving a jagged pink scar across his torso as a reminder of the fight. Then King Corydon arrived at his door.

"Greetings, Conall. I hope you are well," King Corydon began after entering Conall's home. He dismissed the healer, sending her back to the castle, and took a seat in the living room as if he owned it.

"Yes, Your Majesty." Conall nodded.

"Good, that means you are able to return to your service. I need you to go negotiate peace with the Seelie court as my first in command. You may take a small group of soldiers and an advisor with you, but you must leave immediately. We do not want a war, and I have a feeling Casimir may have just started one with his latest rage." Corydon sighed. "I did not think he would care much about losing Ianthe, but I suppose she had a way of getting to all of us, didn't she?" He gave Conall a rare glance of affection at the mention of his daughter.

"Yes sir, I think she did." He and Ianthe may not have had everyone fooled as well as he thought.

"I'm glad you were able to escort her home, and that she arrived safely. I trust we can put this matter behind us and return to how things were before." Corydon smiled tightly.

"As you wish, Your Majesty."

"Wonderful, then you shall leave for the Seelie Court tomorrow morning. Choose your soldiers wisely, and I trust that you will keep the peace."

"Of course." Conall paused. "Sire, do you know if Ianthe…" He trailed off, unsure of how to proceed.

"She is fine. She's safe in her aunt's care and is adjusting back into her life, just as we should. She is no longer of your concern, Conall," Corydon replied tightly, effectively dismissing Conall's ideas for immediately going after her.

"Yes, Your Majesty."

The king stood and strode toward the door. "Very well, I will see you before you and your company leave tomorrow to give you all the details." He exited with those parting words.

Conall knew it would probably be best for everyone if he could pretend Corydon was right and Ianthe was no longer his concern, but he knew that would never be true. She would always be his concern because she owned his heart. He didn't know how or when, but someday he would find his way back to her.

Acknowledgments

First, I'd like to thank my amazing husband, Hassan. I don't think I could have finished this book without your encouragement, support, and steadfast faith in me. You are most definitely my better half and I couldn't have done this without you. Team C and H, baby!

Thank you to my amazing beta girls: Haley Wolf, Callie Vestal, Anna Pertsovsky, Tonya Shaw, and my seester, Kristann Monaghan. Your insights, edits, and suggestions are invaluable and I owe a piece of this book to all of you.

Autumn Doughton, thank you for taking the time to beta read in the very beginning. Your experience, advice, and patience with my never-ending questions are the reason it is the book it is today. I could never repay you for your help. Thank you, thank you, thank you!

Thank you Jo Lowe for taking a chance on me and first publishing me with InknBeans Press. I hope you can read this in heaven while sipping on your coffee. You are missed.

Murphy, you are AMAZING! No, seriously. Your covers are phenomenal (just like your talent). It's like you read my mind to come up with them.

To my mom and dad, thank you for sculpting me into the voracious reader I am today. I love you both!

Colleen Hoover, your words started this all. No, really. I owe this to you. When you said, "Just start writing," I did.

To Sara Ney, Teagan Hunter, Jeramey Kraatz, Chelsea Mueller, and my minxes thank you for your advice, for taking time to answer all of my questions, and your willingness to help me through this whole crazy process.

Thank you Caitlin for your amazing edits and helping me elevate my story (as well as correcting my overuse of that).

To my amazingly supportive friends and family (I don't know where I'd be without your support.

To my previous teachers, I owe you the world. I know how hard your job is, and thank you for making me the writer I am today.

To my students past and present, this is proof that you, too, can achieve your dreams.

To all the authors who came before me, whose books I've devoured and loved, thank you for writing those stories.

To my readers who've been there since the beginning, who cherish the now unicorns, the first books of the Fae Realm (*Ianthe, Return to Fae, and Ayanna*), thank you. I hope these rewrites make you fall in love all over again.

And of course, to you, dear reader: thank you for taking the time to read Ianthe's story. I hope you enjoyed it as much I loved writing it.

About the Author

Cathlin Shahriary lives in Dallas, Texas, with her husband, surrounded by cats (two of which she calls her own) and a 80-pound pitbull puppy named Erwin. By day she is an elementary school teacher, creating future book nerds and writers. By night (and weekends and summer), she is an avid reader, fan girl, author stalker, cat fosterer, and writer.

She hopes this book will be the first of many. You can follow Cathlin on Instagram and Twitter @cshahriary. If you wish to discuss all things Winchester/*Supernatural* or see what she is fan-girling over most recently, you can find her on Facebook at https://www.facebook.com/authorc-shahriary.

Turn to the next page to get a preview of the second book in the Fae Realm series.

FAE REALM SERIES

BOOK 2

The following is an excerpt from Exile, Cathlin Shahri-ary's second book in the Fae Realm series

CHAPTER 1

Conall

IT'S BEEN 7 *days, 8 hours, and 23 Fae minutes since I last saw her beautiful face, since I last gazed into her gorgeous violet eyes, my beautiful Ianthe...not that I am counting or anything.* Conall sighed as thoughts of her swirled through his mind. He had tried countless times to reach her in the dream realm, but just like the first time he had returned to Fae after meeting her, he'd found it to be impossible. Conall recalled that Ianthe was able to visit with her aunt in her dreams while she stayed at the palace in Fae, but he suspected it was only due to their shared bloodline, or perhaps the fact that human minds were easier to manipulate than those of the Fae. Perhaps her powers weren't strong enough to breach the realms yet, although it was always difficult to tell with half Fae. Ianthe's powers might continue to develop, or this could be a permanent limitation. His every thought seemed to center on her, and he missed her as if a portion of his own heart was gone. The truth of that statement struck a chord deep within him.

A portion of his heart was gone.

He had given it to her.

He surmised that she must worry about him and the way things had ended. He'd tried to send word to her with Alfie, his old tutor and confidant, before he left. He stole away the morning of his departure to speak with Alfie in private, and Alfie assured him he would do his best to get his message to Ianthe. He was the only one Conall could trust. Conall wished King Corydon hadn't sent him on a mission so quickly so he could have told Ianthe what was going on and shown her that he was okay. He guessed he had Casimir to thank for that. Stupid, foolish Casimir. Apparently, after their confrontation in the woods, Casimir had gone on a rage-filled rampage, picking fights with anyone within reach, including some Seelie soldiers, and now Conall was the one who had to smooth things over. Hopefully, after this mission, he could request leave. He yearned to return to his beloved every day, and he worried she may doubt his love the longer he stayed away.

Conall shook his head, trying to dislodge his thoughts of Ianthe and instead refocus on his mission. His company, which included several of his most loyal soldiers and the king's advisor, Drummond, was moments away from crossing the Seelie border, and he needed to be on high alert. He knew that even though they came to discuss peace, Casimir's actions would have put the Seelie on edge. "All right lads, be on the lookout for any Seelie. Even though we've come to negotiate peace, that does not mean they will be peaceful in the beginning. Only defensive maneuvers allowed." At that comment, a couple of the soldiers groaned, but he pressed on. "We do not want to exacerbate the situation into a full-blown war. Avoid physical confrontation if at all possible." Drummond gave his nod of approval, and Conall waited for the men to meet his eyes, acknowledging his orders. He would not have anyone under his command make the situation ahead of them any more difficult. After a short pause, they all bowed their heads or nodded to acknowledge his orders.

He pulled his horse to the front of the company and trotted farther down the dirt road, crossing into Seelie territory. He knew it wouldn't be long until they encountered someone. He just hoped whoever they met had been informed of his mission and would not attack or provoke his men. While he was the first in command, he was no king, and his men were Unseelie soldiers who thrived on violence with every bone in their body. The men progressed deeper into Seelie territory, heading through the woods toward the Seelie king's castle. A snap to Conall's left brought him up short. He yanked on the reins of his horse and raised his hand to halt his men. Several swords were drawn within a heartbeat as they paused to see what was to come next. Within moments, Seelie soldiers stepped into the sunlight to Conall's left, followed by others inching forward to his right. Without even realizing it, his men had been surrounded.

"Greetings warriors, I have been sent by King Corydon to discuss peace with King Lachlan. We do not wish a confrontation on our journey." Conall spoke calmly and with authority.

One Seelie warrior brought his horse through the encroaching circle of soldiers. His steed was black as night, matching the hair upon his head, which shone against his deeply tanned skin and amber eyes. He looked as deadly as the aura that surrounded him. Had Conall not known he was Seelie, he would have sworn the knight craved the fight in front of him, but most Seelie were peaceful people. The soldiers parted ways, allowing the dark warrior to pass, an action that reinforced Conall's belief in his authority over the soldiers.

"No confrontation, you say?" The warrior scoffed, his cocky voice interrupting the silence that had fallen among. "Maybe you should have told that to Casimir before he slaughtered my brother." The Seelie surrounding Conall's company drew their swords as the tension grew among all of the warriors from both parties.